Pieces of Me Everywhere

~

REGINA FELTY

To all the young people (and not so young!) who are still trying to figure it all out and feel like an odd puzzle piece that doesn't fit anywhere.

It's okay to be different.

In fact, it can be a beautiful thing.

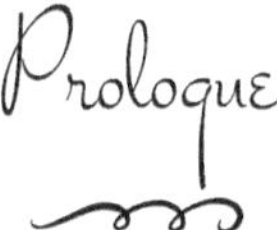

Prologue

Nonna Mancini always told me, "Wisdom is the daughter of experience." But I thought it was just some weird saying she made up.

You know how nonnas are: always clucking their tongue over one infraction or another and trying to scare us by saying things like, "Cracking your knuckles will give you arthritis," and, "If you swallow gum, it takes seven years to digest."

Then, my English teacher told me that Nonna's quote was from Leonardo da Vinci, and I was a bit more impressed. I mean, the guy was a genius. He knew things.

But it wasn't until I'd made a series of bad choices and experienced the consequences of them that Nonna's quote made perfect sense.

I learned a lot of wisdom that year. The year I was seventeen.

Chapter One

"Tessa, stop laughing! The whole neighborhood's gonna hear you! Let's get out of here," I hiss into Tessa's ear, who's tumbled into me and knocked us both back into the middle of the bush we'd been crouched in front of, a branch now entangled in my long braid.

It's bad enough that the neighbor's rottweiler-on-steroids has been snarling at us—hackles raised, teeth bared—from the back fence for the past ten minutes. I would too if I were a dog and two strangers were hiding in the bushes behind my property.

I can't believe I'm even out here doing this. I'm not the type of person to sneak around on other peoples' properties, but Tessa always gets us into these messes. Of course, I'm dumb enough to always go along with her ideas.

Tessa finally stifles her obnoxious giggling, sits up, and picks a thorn out of her elbow. Then, she has the nerve to grin at me. "Oh, come on, Alli. Brent hasn't come out yet. I didn't sneak out and risk my neck just to see Rick and Cindi make out in the grass and some dude barf in the planter. All the real action is *inside* the house! Let's see if we can get closer."

Tessa starts to stand up, but I yank her back down by her jacket sleeve, nearly toppling us both over again.

Steroid dog escalates from giving us warning growls to barking. That's my cue to beat it out of there before he gives us away. "Nope, Tessa. I'm not doing it. That's all the excitement I can handle for one night. I'm going home," I announce. It's my turn to make a move, and my destination is back the way we came before we made this stupid decision to check out Chad's party.

Tessa and I glance once more back at the house, where we notice several upstairs lights start coming on.

"Fine," she huffs, trailing behind me as we make our way home.

The dog works himself into a frenzy as I hurry Tessa along and worry about how I'm going to sneak back into the house without getting caught.

Chapter Two

EVER SINCE LUNCH, Tessa has such an attitude.

All because I didn't wait for her when the lunch bell rang. Sheesh, I was starving and didn't get breakfast this morning. Tessa never misses breakfast, so she doesn't get it. Plus, they were serving cheese crisps—my favorite.

For science class, Tessa picks Brynne to partner with her for labs and hasn't said one word to me since class started.

Whatever.

Zach's the closest body next to me when I overhear Tessa ask Brynne, so I tag him in. "Hey, Zach, you want to be my lab partner?"

Zach isn't a guy I normally notice—that anyone really notices, now that I think of it—but he's the fastest solution for me to save face in case Tessa glances this way. He looks like he would rather stick his head in a blender than partner with me, but I don't give him a chance to think about it. I need him right now.

"Pleeease, Zach, I need a partner."

Please say yes, please say yes.

Zach blinks frantically as he peers over at Tessa, who he knows is normally my partner. I'm sure he's going to bail on me.

"Uh . . . yeah, sure. I guess so."

I could hug him, which would be the last thing on earth I would ever consider doing. I grace him with a beaming smile instead. "Cool!"

I sound way too excited and, by the puzzled look on his face, Zach isn't buying it. Afraid he might change his mind, I say, "I'll go grab the lab supplies." I'm up and heading to the supply table to get the things we need before he can say anything.

As I walk up, I notice that Brynne's already at the table collecting tubes and eyedroppers for the project. I slow my pace on purpose to look casual so that, you know, Brynne thinks I couldn't care less about the partner switch today.

"What's up, Alli?" she asks as I come up to the table.

I plaster on a fake smile and act surprised to see her. "Oh, hey, Brynne. What's up?"

"Do you know where the extra goggles are?" She holds up two pairs. "The straps on these are broken."

I feel like telling her to ask her *partner,* Tessa, but I don't. It's not her fault that Tessa's using her to get back at me. Instead, I point to a black crate on a shelf that lines the back wall. "Yeah, over there."

From the corner of my eye, I notice Tessa looking our way.

She's trying not to make eye contact with me, pretending all her attention is on Brynne, but I'm not dumb.

Since I have an audience, I decide to make a show of it. I snatch a few tubes and an eyedropper and march—more like *sway*—over to where Zach waits patiently, chewing on a thumbnail, his biology notebook and several mechanical pencils studiously laid out in front of him.

I peek to make sure Tessa's still watching and let out a laugh loud enough for her to hear so she'll think Zach and I are sharing a private joke or something. Then, in a lower voice, I point to Zach's organized ensemble.

"Gee, Zach, are we planning to analyze the entire nuclear fusion process today or something?" It's the first time I've ever seen Zach smile before. He actually has a nice smile.

"I doubt *you* were going to take any notes," he says, sliding his notebook closer to him. Then, he stands and starts to set up the supplies for our experiment.

Ouch. I have to hand it to him; he's right.

Tessa usually takes notes for science while I entertain her with the latest drama I've picked up in my first period class, world history. My world history teacher, Mr. Ankor, is a hipster who sits at his desk every day and peers over his laptop at us as he munches on organic kale chips. His greeting never changes as we file into class: "Today's worksheet"—and it's always a work-sheet— "is on the back table. Find your seat and get to work."

Needless to say, no one gets any serious work done during the fifty minutes we're stuck in there. So Ankor's class is where I catch up on the latest gossip and on who's having a party at their house that weekend. The gossip is something juicy to pass on to Tessa, even though I wouldn't dare go to those kinds of parties myself, where I'm sure a lot of less-than-legal things go on.

It's not just the parties. There are quite a few things I choose to keep my distance from.

I'm a Christian. A born and bred Apostolic Pentecostal girl, which means I don't look like the other girls at school because I only wear dresses and skirts and have long hair.

There's more to my faith than my clothes and hair, but that's what many people notice first about me—and the part I struggle with the most at times. I love God and all, but I'm still figuring some things out about life, so I'm not always the best version of a pristine, Christian girl.

Which is why Tessa and I ended up sneaking out and spying on Chad's party Friday night.

I pull my attention back to what I'm supposed to be doing right now: helping Zach. Tugging open my backpack, I start digging around for my notebook.

Where is it? It was in here yesterday...

Then, I remember. Tessa has it. She borrowed it to copy my lab notes yesterday (even though, true to my reputation, I hadn't written much) because she'd been called to the office for something and missed most of science class.

What seriously irks me is that she *knows* she has my notebook. I saw her book out when I passed her table, and I know she had to see mine next to hers when she pulled it out of her backpack.

I toss my backpack on the floor and stand up. "Hey, Zach.

Um, I need to grab my notebook from Tessa. Be right back."

Zach doesn't even look up. He's busy measuring baking soda into a tube. "Yeah, okay."

I feel like the worst lab partner in all West Morrison High School while I walk over to Tessa's table. She has a bored look on her face as she watches me. I ignore it.

"Tessa, I need my science notebook."

Brynne looks at me, then over at Tessa. She probably wonders why Tessa partnered with her instead of me. And by the look on her face while she observes the tension between Tessa and I, it's probably starting to dawn on her that she was only a pawn to get back at me.

"I don't have your notebook, Alli," Tessa says.

The puzzled look on Tessa's face almost convinces me that she's telling the truth. Almost. *Yeah, right.*

Brynne takes the tension between me and Tessa as her hint to leave and chat with her friend, Candace, who's sitting three tables away.

I take Brynne's vacated seat and plant myself across from Tessa. "Really, Tessa? What's your problem? Are you really that bent at me for not waiting for you at lunch?" I throw my hands in the air. "I ran ahead to the front of the line before all the cafeteria vultures showed up. You know how long that line gets! I would've caught up with you like I always do after I grab my food, so I don't get what you're so worked up over."

I feel better confronting Tessa about her being so immature. Maybe she'll see how juvenile it sounds hearing me say it straight.

"Well," Tessa flicks her ponytail back and leans in close,

sarcasm dripping from every word, "I guess your cheese crisp must've been *super* important because I told you this morning that something happened last night that I wanted to tell you about during lunch. You couldn't wait five more minutes for me?" She shook her head. "Sad, Alli. I hope the cheese crisp was worth it."

Oh, no, I didn't . . . how did I . . . ?

Wow. I feel awful. Seven times worse than awful. How could I have forgotten that Tessa wanted to talk to me? She sent a text this morning saying some bad things were going down at home and her parents had called a family meeting last night with her and her brother, Aaron.

No wonder she's miffed that I stood her up for cheese crisps. I mean, I wasn't even in line that long, but still . . .

My superior attitude deflates to the size of a shriveled balloon, and I give Tessa my most convincing I'm-the-worst-best-friend-ever look. "Tessa, I'm *so* sorry. I feel so bad!"

She shrugs and inspects one of her fingernails like my mistake is no more of a big deal than a smudge on her sunglasses, but I know Tessa better than that.

"Whatever," she says. "It's cool."

I'm about to launch into another lame apology when the bell rings. "Wait up," I say. "Let me grab my—"

But Tessa's already throwing her backpack over her shoulder and walking away. She hasn't even bothered to put her science notebook in her backpack; it's tucked against her chest as she brushes pass Brynne, who's just coming back to grab her stuff.

"Oh, hey, Tessa," Brynne calls out. "Do you want—"

But Tessa's left the building. Well, the classroom, at least.

I don't wait around, because I can't afford to be late to my next class, English Literature. Mrs. Monroe—as in Marilyn Monroe, except this teacher's no curvy, blonde bombshell with a flirty grin—would fix those beady eyes of hers on me and hand me a detention slip without so much as a hiccup in her opening speech.

Mrs. Monroe, English Lit Extraordinaire, is pushing probably seventy (and that's a conservative guess) and has a puff of white hair resembling a bird's nest after a windstorm that sits primly on top of her head. She's always yelling about something, although her hollering comes out sounding more like an owl with strep throat.

She also walks around with a perpetual scowl on her wrinkled face, and I have to wonder if she was once a sweet, eager young teacher who got all hyped about dissecting a piece of literature the same way our science teacher, Mr. Martin, was all into cutting into toads last semester.

Did she finally start to catch on after a decade (*or is it two?*) of dealing with unruly high school kids who maybe just weren't into English Lit the way she was?

I sprint down the long hall, weaving around couples embracing for one last moment before class and loafers who make it a point to defy the late bell. I'm still worrying about how I can make things up to Tessa for being such a jerk and abandoning her. Then, the bells rings.

I realize something else and, suddenly, Mrs. Monroe and Tessa aren't my only worries. "Great," I mumble, slowing my pace. "I dumped Zach too."

Chapter Three

"THANKS again to all of you who showed up Friday to help paint the recreation center at Brookstone," Brother McGuire announces after youth class. "The director called this morning and wanted me to let you all know that the residents really appreciate how nice the center looks. I'm very proud of the difference you're making in our community. Good work!"

"Glad to help, boss," one guy in the back of the room calls out, which starts everyone laughing.

I nod and smile along with them but, to be honest, I'm a little distracted right now. Painting Brookstone's rec center with the youth group had been loads of fun, and I like volunteering for the local community and all, but what I did later that night makes me feel like a loser.

It's my fault to start with, really. I was the one who told Tessa about Chad's party Friday night after overhearing a group of guys talking about it in class.

Naturally, she was all over it. "Oh, Alli, let's go check it out," she begged me. "Chad lives a few blocks over from us. It would be an easy walk. You could meet at my place, then we can sneak over and spy the party from the back of his house. There's a huge, empty lot back there with a bunch of over-grown bushes and stuff where we can hide."

I tried to douse the fire I'd sparked. "No way, Tessa. What am I supposed to tell my mom, 'Hey, Mom, I'm going for a walk'—which I *never* do— 'to get some fresh air? Go ahead and go to bed because I'll be gone for an hour or so?'" I laugh. "Yeah, I'm sure that would go over really well. Besides, my youth group is helping out at Brookstone that night and I promised to be there."

"Alli, you'll be done at Brookstone way before the party's even really getting started. The heavy stuff doesn't start happening until after midnight," she tells me. "Your mom will probably be in bed hours before that."

Tessa should seriously think about becoming a defense attorney instead of the veterinarian she claims she wants to become someday. She's the most persuasive person I know when it comes to her wild ideas. Unfortunately, I'm usually the one she tries to persuade.

My mom says that Tessa's an "instigator" and that I have no backbone when it comes to stuff she talks me into doing. It kind of hurts my feelings when she says that, but I can't deny that she's right.

That's how Tessa and I ended up hiding in the bushes behind Chad's house at one o'clock in the morning, and why all the good feels I had from painting the rec center and making a bunch of old people happy drain out of me one painful drip at a time with every word of praise Brother McGuire lavishes on our youth group.

"Hey, Alli," a voice whispers near the back of my head.

When I turn to look, I notice it's Kristin. I try not to roll my eyes.

"What, Kristin?" I growl back.

A few others look our way. I scrunch my eyebrows, so it looks like I'm concentrating on what Brother McGuire is saying instead of rudely having a side conversation.

"Got any gum?" she asks.

I'm not even going to give her the courtesy of wasting my voice on her, so I stare straight ahead and shake my head. The nerve of her to ask me for gum in the middle of youth class. *Since when do we chew gum in youth class anyway?*

Finally, after what seems like an eternity, Brother McGuire asks Anthony to lead the group in prayer to close the meeting. I bow my head and close my eyes. I pray along with Anthony, adding my own words to his under my breath: "God, please forgive me for sneaking out Friday night. Do I have to confess to my mom?"

"Alli!"

The patter of sandals hitting the linoleum grows louder right before a heavy thud hits my desk and scares me half to death. My science notebook stares up at me.

I look up at Tessa's glowing face hovering above me. She

fans herself with one hand, tugs her shirt down with the other, and taps one foot. She's so animated that it's like someone plugged her into the electrical outlet behind her. I'm totally confused. Yesterday, it was all about dirty looks and stone silence from her, but now, she looks completely thrilled to see me.

"Uh . . . hi, Tessa." I glance down at the book on my desk. "Thanks for remembering my notebook."

The chair next to mine scrapes across the bare floor as Tessa pulls up close to me and throws her bag on the floor. The new highlights in her auburn hair shimmer when her ponytail swats against me as she plops down.

I glance around the study hall, noticing that the large room is empty except for the two of us.

Well, I guess that means she's definitely here to see me.

In case there's any room for doubt, Tessa grabs my arm. "Guess what!" She doesn't wait for my answer, which is a classic Tessa habit. "Kim just told me I made the cheer team!" Tessa bit her lip and paused. "Well, it's not official yet because they haven't posted the names, but she wanted to give me a heads up." Tessa starts bouncing in her chair. "Eek! I'm so nervous!"

This is where I guess I'm supposed to jump up and hug my best friend, and we're supposed to squeal and carry on together over her exciting announcement. But I don't.

I glance around the room once more for confirmation.

Yep, she's talking to me.

"Wait, Tessa," I hold up a hand to get her attention, which is hard to do because she's a bundle of squirmy jitters next to me. "I don't get it. Yesterday, you wouldn't even talk to me, and—"

"Oh, I'm over that, Alli," she interrupts, yesterday's ordeal going up in a puff of forgotten smoke. "Aren't you happy for me?"

She waits for my approval and for me to jump on the happiness trampoline with her, but my thoughts are still misfiring.

"Um, alright, Tessa. You're over it; I get it. But I thought you were only trying out for cheer so you could meet the football players who were hanging out at the tryouts. I didn't think you were *serious*." I pause, trying to absorb Tessa's announcement. "And . . . who's Kim?"

Two boys and a girl drift into the room, and the clock mounted on the wall above our heads shows that we have two minutes before the first-period bell rings.

Tessa notices too and grabs her bag as she slides off the chair. "Kim's the cheer captain." She waves her hand impatiently, as if that trivial detail is a fly she's batting out of her face. "Anyhow, I didn't really think I would make it, Alli. I was kind of only trying out for fun, but after the first practice day, I felt like I could really do it."

Tessa smiles at the girl now looking our way and lowers her voice. "I went home and watched the YouTube videos of the cheers Kim uploaded and practiced them over and over until Aaron banged on my door and said I was getting on his nerves with all the pounding." Tessa giggles. "It got me all excited to *really* do this, and . . . I made it!" She turns and starts running just as the bell rings. "Gotta go!"

"Whoa, what in the world just happened?"

The two boys look over at me, and I realize I've said that out loud. I grab my backpack and run (why does it always feel like I'm running to every class?) to first period, even though Mr. Ankor never notices who comes or goes in his class.

I don't care if they serve cheese crisps—or even prime rib at this point—for lunch today. I'll be looking for Tessa as soon as the lunch bell rings. We need to talk.

Chapter Four

I stare at Tessa across the table, nibbling on the corner of a limp slice of cafeteria pizza that makes Little Caesars seem like gourmet food.

Tessa's been going on for ten minutes about upcoming cheer practices and how she's going to need to go to the tanning salon so she doesn't look like a ghost in her uniform when it arrives in a few weeks.

"The cheer uniforms cost *four hundred dollars*! Can you believe it? Where am I going to get four hundred dollars? My parents . . . well, let's just say it's not the best time to bring it up."

Tessa sighs and takes a big gulp of her energy drink. We aren't allowed to have energy drinks at school, but Tessa doesn't care. She sneaks one in her bag every day to drink at lunch. She claims she needs the caffeine boost to get her through the rest of the afternoon.

"Are you sure you want to even do this, Tessa?" I give her

my best concerned-best-friend stare. "Remember when you wanted to play guitar in seventh grade, and you paid two hundred bucks for a guitar that you got tired of carrying around after two weeks?" I ask.

From a glance down at my cell phone, I see that we only have fifteen minutes left of lunch, and this isn't how I'd planned for the conversation to go. I'd been hoping Tessa would spit out what happened when her parents called that meeting with her and Aaron.

I have a dentist appointment after school and Bible study at church tonight, and I really don't want to hear about it in a text, because Tessa's a much better talker than texter. She'd leave out all the important stuff if she had to text it all out, and I'm the kind of person who needs every detail when you tell me something so I can picture it all in my head.

Tessa reaches over, grabs the discarded pizza crust from my tray, tears off a chunk, and chews it loudly—which is kind of one of my pet peeves, but whatever. She looks over at a table of guys next to us and makes eye contact with one of the better-looking ones of the group, who happens to be staring at her. She swallows the pizza crust and turns back to me.

"Yeah, I remember that guitar, but this is different, Alli. I mean, at first, I wasn't all that serious about cheerleading because, I don't know, I guess I just never thought about it. But it was kind of fun challenging myself to learn the cheers and moves and then to compete against the other girls who were trying out." Tessa shrugs.

"I wanted to see if I could actually do it. And it really happened, Alli. I made it! I'm super excited about it now . . .

except I don't know how I'm going to pay for the uniform and all. I think I need new shoes and a duffle bag too." She frowns and tosses the rest of the crust back onto my tray.

I'm completely confused. In all the years Tessa's been my best friend, we've always made fun of the popular girls who made a big deal over designer clothes and went through best friends like revolving doors. Tessa and I always preferred to spend our weekends scouring thrift stores and yard sales for cool finds. *Two bucks for an outdated Fossil purse? Score!*

One time, Tessa walked over to my house in her bathrobe and slippers to do homework because she was too lazy to get dressed. Let's just say Tessa's the *last* person I would picture as the cheerleader type.

I give her my best "You're joking, right?" stare before I ask, "How *are* you going to come up with the money, Tessa? Are your parents even going to go for this? I mean, don't they have to sign some kind of permission form, and are your grades even up to par?"

Tessa glares at me. "This isn't middle school, Alli. My grades are fine, and I don't think my parents have to sign anything unless I'm going off-campus, like if we travel to another school or out of town. Which we will . . ." Tessa's eyebrows scrunch as she considers it. "Man, I hope they take us to the games on a bus or something because my parents will never drive me." She looks worried.

I take this as a perfect time to jump in. "Yeah, about that. What happened with that meeting your parents had with you and Aaron?" I push my lunch tray to the side so I can lean in closer. It's hard to keep Tessa's attention for long, and I want to make sure I lock it in while I can.

Tessa looks down and starts to pick at her nail polish, her frown deepening.

Uh oh, this doesn't look good.

"Oh, it was nothing important. They were just getting on us about some stuff. It's all cool." Tessa's face looks blotchy—a lot like how she looks before she's going to cry.

I start blinking because if my best friend is about to cry, I'm going to be doing it with her, even if I don't know what we're crying about yet. "You're lying, Tessa," I say.

She looks up at me, then takes a deep breath. "Yeah, I am. But . . . I don't want to talk about it right now. Okay?"

I grab her hand and give it a big squeeze. "Alright, Tes. I understand. I'm here when you're ready to talk."

It's the last thing I want to say, because the curiosity is killing me. But I'm a big girl, so I say it anyway.

I'VE NEVER BEEN good at taking tests, and today's science quiz only proves the point.

I skip the questions I'm not sure about, hoping to go back to them last. But that's not proving to be helpful at all, because I'm staring at a page with seven out of twenty questions answered. The answers are all multiple choice, but if I end up guessing all the others wrong, I'll only have a thirty-five percent for a grade. Basically, a glaring *fail*.

It doesn't help that we have to sit on these hundred-year-old metal, barstool-style chairs and that I'm bent over the table at an unnatural angle that's killing my back.

I squirm and peek over at Tessa across the table. She senses me looking and sticks her tongue out at me. Even though it irks me that she probably knows all the answers and will earn a perfect grade, I smile and stick my tongue out back at her.

Tessa, Brynne, Zach, and I sit together at one table now since Tessa and I made up. Brynne and I get the most benefit out of the deal. Since Tessa and Zach are both organized and smart, we're more than happy to be the errand girls—grabbing the supplies we need and doing the cleanup afterward—while Zach and Tessa set up the experiments, make notes of the data collected, and do all the technical stuff that Brynne and I couldn't care less about. Which is why I'm struggling with this quiz right now.

When Mr. Martin announces that he'll be collecting our quizzes in ten minutes, I start the guessing game with the rest of the questions, making false promises to myself under my breath that I *will* do better in this class. I circle my last choice, toss my pencil on the table, and slap the test facedown just as Mr. Martin calls out, "Time!"

Zach's already standing and reaching for our papers. He's always done first anyway, so I guess that makes him the designated test collector.

"How do you think you did?" Brynne asks. I think she meant the question for both Tessa and me, but Tessa is rummaging through her backpack for something and not paying attention.

Since I'm looking right at Brynne, I answer. "Eh, I guess I

did okay." I'm not really lying; I'm just having faith that I was a lucky guesser.

Mr. Martin starts talking about the new unit he'll be introducing tomorrow, and Brynne turns away. I slide my cell phone from my pocket and, even though Tessa's sitting right across from me, I text her to ask if she wants to go to Tucson Mall after school. I don't want Brynne to overhear.

The trill of a young Michael Jackson singing, "I'll be There," blares from the other side of the table.

I force a cough to stop myself from laughing. Tessa forgot to silence her phone again.

As I wait for Tessa to freak out, trying to silence her phone before Mr. Martin notices and confiscates it, Shanice walks up, and Tessa tosses the phone in her backpack, the best-friend ringtone ignored. Tessa stares up at Shanice like a hopeless fangirl, giving Shanice her undivided attention and nodding her head to whatever she's saying.

Since when does Shanice ever show her face around our half of the classroom? I wonder.

That's when it hits me: Shanice is co-captain of the cheer squad, and Tessa just recently made the team.

This should be interesting.

When the bell rings, I throw my backpack over my shoulder and move toward Tessa, waiting for her to wrap it up with Shanice, roll her eyes as soon as Shanice walks away, and give me the scoop on the way to third period.

But it doesn't happen that way.

Zach has a front-row view of me standing in shock as Tessa gets up and walks off with Shanice. I catch him looking and know what he's thinking—well, I imagine I know since I ran out on him as my partner a few days ago: *See how it feels?*

I CORNER TESSA outside her third period dance class.

"Wow, Tessa. What was that even about?"

I only have a minute because I don't plan to be late to English Lit again, but I'm irritated and want to get it off my chest while I have the chance.

"What, Alli? Shanice was telling me about practice on Thursday. What's your problem?"

"My *problem* is that you and everyone else in class heard my text, but you ignored it. Then, you walk off with Shanice and don't even wait for me. What's the deal? We always walk to class together."

Tessa acts chill, looking at me like I'm a toddler throwing a tantrum in the grocery store. Like snubbing me in science was no big deal.

That only makes me madder.

"Oh, my gosh, Alli," she says. "Stop being so dramatic. She came up right when my phone went off. I was going to text you back when I got to my next class."

Okay, so maybe I was being a bit dramatic. I don't know why I'm making a big deal out of her talking to other people. We've never been jealous and territorial over each other like that. I have to backtrack out of this so I can get to class and so Tessa doesn't spend the next hour thinking her best friend is a psychopath.

The air seeps from my lungs like slashed tires as my ego deflates. "Sorry. I guess I *am* overreacting a little."

She raises an eyebrow. "A little?"

I sock her in the arm. "Seriously, Tessa. *Shanice?* I know you're in cheer now, but she was acting like you two are friends now or something." I snort. "Like that would ever happen."

Judging by the look on Tessa's face, she doesn't agree.

"She's not a monster, Alli. Shanice is pretty cool, actually. You just have to get to know her."

"Yeah, that's about as likely to happen as Tucson becoming a ski resort," I say, backing away so I can make a run to class before the bell.

"Well, she's been nicer than you've been so far this morning."

I know she won't hear me because she's already walking into class, but I respond anyway. "Well, maybe she'll offer to buy that four-hundred-dollar cheer uniform for you since she's so *nice*."

I make it to English Lit and into my seat before the bell, bubbling with frustration over the science quiz I'm sure I bombed and Tessa's snotty attitude. *I even apologized!*

When my phone vibrates in my skirt pocket a few minutes later, I smile. I knew Tessa would smooth things over.

I slide my phone out just far enough to see the notification at the top of the screen, expecting a goofy emoji to make me smile. Instead, it's Tessa's reply to my earlier text about shopping later on:

Can't make it tonight.

I hit the delete button.

Fine, I fume. *I don't want to be around you right now anyway.*

To add to my great morning, Mrs. Monroe yells at the class for being loud and for not having our notebooks out and ready for class.

Maybe I'll go sit in the library during lunch.

Chapter Five

I FIND OUT THAT, instead of going to Tucson Mall with me last night, Tessa met up with the cheer team at Kim's house—Kim, the cheer captain who basically rules over her little pom-pom-toting minions like a queen over her subjects. I've seen them walking around campus, following her like ducklings in a row. It's pathetic.

I guess they met to go over plans for the season and hang out. I don't know why Tessa didn't just tell me that instead of sending me that lame text when I invited her to hang out.

Why didn't she *want* to tell me?

I'm pretty sure I already know two reasons why. One, she didn't want to hear a lecture from me about how dumb I think the cheerleading idea is since Tessa couldn't have cared less about cheerleading a month ago. Two—and this one kind of hurts—she wanted to be with them more than she wanted to be with me.

In fact, I only found out about the whole thing because

Avery, my nine-year-old sister (who's really my cousin—a story for another time), goes to school with one of the younger sisters of another girl on the cheer team, and that sister told Avery about the get-together. I know it sounds like I'm being a stalker, but I'm really trying to figure out why my best friend is being all secretive and snobby all of a sudden.

I don't feel bad about stalking her either.

At the dinner table with my family, curious vibes pervade the air, and I catch glances of the side-eyes from Mom and Dad. Even Avery shoots warning looks my way. I eat faster to hopefully avoid the twenty questions I know they're all dying to ask.

"So, Alli, you're quiet tonight. Everything okay?"

I should have known that Dad would start the inter-rogation.

Too late. I shove a spoonful of minestrone soup in my mouth and reach for a dinner roll. When I notice that I already have one on my napkin—*Good one, Alli*—I toss the new one back in the basket. Mom doesn't even bring up the "you touched it, you eat it" line, so I know all the focus is on me right now.

I look across the table at my dad and widen my eyes like I just realized he was talking to me. "Oh, yeah. Everything's fine. I guess I don't feel much like talking tonight."

Mom's turn.

"Did you have a bad day today? You aren't usually this quiet at dinner."

Why didn't I remember that the "I don't feel like talking"

excuse always sets off parental alarms? I whip my eyes over to Avery in a silent plea for interference.

Say something, Avery. We normally can't shut you up during dinner.

I dip one edge of my roll in my soup, but before I stick it in my mouth, I give Mom a reassuring smile. "No, it was a normal, boring day. I guess I'm just tired. I'm going to work on an article for the newspaper in my room for a while, and then head to bed early."

To make my point, I bite off the dipped part of my roll and set the rest down even though I'm actually still hungry. I fake a small yawn, stand, and move to start collecting the empty bowls and salad plates to take to the kitchen. Since Mom and Dad work together to make dinner most nights, Avery and I always take care of the cleanup afterward.

When I realize I'm the only one who appears to be done eating, I just grab my bowl and scoop up the empty salad plates from everyone.

Dad butters a roll and stares at me over his glasses, his eyes telling me he doesn't buy my excuse. Dad can always read me and knows when I'm lying.

"You hardly ate anything, Alli," Mom says, a soft sigh escaping her lips. "Leave the dishes. Avery and I will take care of them. You go finish up and get a decent night's rest."

I'm sure guilt is written all over my face. "Alright. Thanks, Mom. I'll at least take my stuff to the kitchen. Dinner was great tonight, by the way."

I spin around and head to the kitchen, avoiding Avery's bewildered look. I don't know if she's pitying me or if she's upset that I'm abandoning her with our parents for the rest of the meal.

While I rinse my bowl and salad plate, I hear her start talking about the substitute teacher she had in class today and how the sub spent the whole day trying to get the class under control and even kept them in from recess.

Thanks a lot, Avery. Now you start talking.

"I'LL TAKE a bag of corn nuts and a blueberry muffin, please."

"Alli!"

I whip around just as Tessa races up the sidewalk leading to the snack bar, her sandals slapping the ground and her backpack swinging over one shoulder. Her keys are still in her hand.

"Grab me a snack!"

I turn back to the guy taking my order. He's holding the muffin as if he's not sure if I'm about to change my mind.

"Make that *two* blueberry muffins," I say.

Tessa bends over her backpack on the ground, shoving her keys into a side pocket, then checking the time on her phone.

I pay for our food and hold the muffin out to her.

"Thanks. I'm a basket case this morning. My alarm didn't go off, and Aaron couldn't find his geometry homework," Tessa says. "I almost just left him."

Tessa eyes the insulated tumbler in my hand while we make our way to a table. "Is that coffee?"

I'm a little reluctant to hand it over even though we've always shared everything. To be truthful, I'm trying to figure out what the deal is. Did she forget she snubbed me yesterday —*twice!*—or was it just my imagination?

I hand the coffee to her.

"Nice spray tan," I say.

She does a little twirl and a bow, which almost throws her off balance when the weight of her backpack shifts. "You like it? Gotta look the new cheerleader part, right?"

It's a bummer she misses the dirty look I give her since she's already on the move to find a place to sit.

We find a table under a tree, and I push the corn nuts down into my backpack for later. Tessa pops the top open on the tumbler and takes a timid sip of the hot liquid. If we bring coffee to school, we usually have to chug it before the bell rings because drinks aren't allowed in class. But I bring an insulated container that keeps my coffee hot for hours so I can sip it when the teachers are distracted and in between class periods.

Unwrapping my muffin, I watch Tessa push the cap of the tumbler back down and pull her muffin closer to her.

"Thanks for the muffin too," she says. "You're a lifesaver. I didn't get a chance to eat before I left the house and I'm starving." She opens the hand sanitizer hooked on the handle of her backpack, squeezes out a blob, and leans it toward me. "Do you need some?"

I shake my head.

She rubs the sanitizer in, lifts her muffin, and takes the first bite. Her eyes roll, and she sighs. "Perfect," she says. Then, she looks at me. "So did you have fun at the mall last night?"

Instead of saying what I'm really thinking: *Oh, you mean the shopping trip you didn't want to go on because you went to hang out with your snobby new friends?* I shrug and say, "I didn't end up going."

"Oh, bummer."

"What did *you* end up doing?" I can't resist. "Other than getting a fresh spray tan." My finger twirls above her imitation-sun-kissed arm.

Having already inhaled her muffin, Tessa grabs the coffee again and takes another sip. "Oh, I had a meeting to go to." She looks down at her arm. "Well, we met first at the salon, then had the meeting." She brushes muffin crumbs off her lap, suddenly avoiding eye contact with me.

"A cheer meeting?"

Tessa looks up at me and I can tell she's trying to read my mood. I don't try to hold back the bad vibes I'm sending her way either.

"Yeah. It was kind of a last-minute thing," she finally says. "Scheduling and stuff."

"Oh, okay," I say. "You don't have to make appointments for salons anymore either?"

"Huh?" She looks down at her golden skin. "Oh, this salon allows walk-ins." She gives me a pointed look. "Why do you have to say it like *that*?"

I sense her becoming defensive, but I'm not having it. Because of her, I barely slept last night.

"Because you knew you had this meeting, and you didn't even tell me when I asked if you wanted to go shopping with me. What's with the secrets all of a sudden, Tessa?"

Tessa drags her backpack onto her lap and rests her chin on the handle. I've known this girl since second grade. When she puts a barrier between us—like her backpack right now or even the gigantic bear she keeps on her bed—that means she's feeling guilty.

"Alright. I'm sorry, Alli," she says. "I did know there was supposed to be some kind of meeting, but I didn't think I needed to be there at first. Shanice is the one who told me." She sighs.

"Actually, after I went," Tessa continues, "we only talked about the cheer schedule for about ten minutes. The rest of the night, they went on about hot guys at school and their latest Netflix binges. I felt totally awkward—like a fish out of water. It was like I didn't even belong there."

"You *don't*, Tessa."

I push my half-eaten muffin to the side and fold my arms on the table, preparing to give her an impromptu pep talk.

"You're nothing like them. In fact, you're *better* than them in a thousand different ways. Look, I know you want to try something new, and I'd be super excited if I was picked for something important like this too. I support whatever you want, but just don't let it change you, girl." I give her shoulder a gentle shove. "Have your fling in short skirts and dorky pom-poms, and then come back down to reality. Okay? Promise?"

Tessa's cheeks flush, and I know I've hit the target. She gives me a grin and, suddenly, all feels better in my world.

"I love you, dork." She giggles.

"I love you more, dummy." I laugh. Then, I notice other kids getting up from the tables and glance down at my watch. The bell's going to ring in two minutes. I push my coffee across the table to Tessa. "Take it. I think you're going to need it more than me this morning."

Just as she reaches for it, Shanice and Kim walk by with a cluster of other girls around them. Kim looks over as they pass our table.

"Hey, Tessa!" she calls out. "Come walk with us."

Tessa locks eyes with me and I see the pleading look, but I don't know how to respond. I shouldn't care who she wants to walk to class with, but the look she's giving me makes me feel like she's either seeking my permission or asking for my help.

But before I can open my mouth—not that I know what I would say—she swings one leg off the bench and pulls her backpack on.

"Be right there!" Tessa grabs the coffee tumbler. "Thanks, Alli. I'll catch you in second period, okay?" She blows me an air kiss and walks over to meet them.

Oh, Tessa . . .

Chapter Six

I don't like being different.

Some people live to stand out in a crowd and leave their footprint in the world, but I'm not like that. I want to blend in and just be another piece of the whole, mundane puzzle.

You know how you dump all the pieces of a new puzzle out onto the table and start making piles of all the similar colors and patterns before you start putting the whole thing together? Maybe that's just how my family and I work through puzzles.

But the best way I can describe myself is that I always feel like someone purposely threw one piece into the box that really belongs to an entirely different puzzle and, when someone starts putting the puzzle together, it's obvious that the piece isn't going to fit anywhere.

The odd puzzle piece? Yeah, that's me.

What was the term we learned in algebra again? Oh, right. *Outlier.* A value that lies *outside* the other values. Which is exactly how I feel most of the time—like I'm on the outside looking in. I still have value; it's just that my value looks different than everyone else's at home, at church, and at school.

Especially at school.

At least with my family and youth group, we all have the same standards, believe the same way, have similar interests and values, and so on because we're all Christians. None of us think twice about saying grace over a meal and going to church three times a week. We all feel the same about dressing modestly and avoiding things that are contrary to our faith. We *get* each other.

I can't say I always follow my faith in my heart *exactly* like I probably should (which is what I mean about my values looking different), but I don't think my family or Christian friends really notice too much.

But at school, I feel like an alien who got dropped off on the wrong planet.

I can't help but sense that I'm always under a microscope. I know there are lots of Christians in my high school, but not all of them believe the same way as I do about modesty standards and things I don't do or places I choose not to go. So, even around other Christians, I still find myself feeling like the one odd duck in the whole pond.

Which is exactly what I *don't* want.

I haven't figured out, decided—whatever—how I feel about my faith yet. I was born in a Christian home, was raised by Christian parents, and have learned to love God for myself. But part of me wants to just blend in sometimes and not stand for anything unique or bear a label that identifies my faith.

As I said, I don't *like* being different.

Chapter Seven

EXCEPT FOR BEFORE school and during lunch—and that's after standing in line forever at the snack bar—I've hardly had any time with Tessa. So, I do what any self-respecting best friend would do: I show up at her house uninvited.

Tessa's mom answers the door, and I can tell right away that she's excited to see me. "Alli! It's so good to see you. Come on in." She moves aside so I can slip past her.

"Thanks, Mrs. Williams. Is, uh, Tessa . . ."

"Oh, go on up. She's in her room. Can you let her know dinner will be ready in about fifteen minutes?" She pulls me into a quick hug. "You can join us too!"

Mrs. Williams is one of the coolest moms I know. She's always cooking something delicious or has an incredible dessert she made sitting out on the counter. If I'm hungry after school, the Williams' house is the first place I stop.

It's not like we don't have food at my house. I mean, we *are* Italian after all. My parents are both amazing cooks and spoil

Avery and me with homemade bread and fresh pasta most nights of the week. I'm amazed that I'm not twenty pounds heavier than I am.

But sometimes, I crave a good, old American hamburger, and the Williams have hamburgers a lot.

"Thank you for the offer," I say, "but I don't plan to stay long. I just wanted to chat with Tessa for a bit."

I make my way up the stairs to Tessa's room like I have hundreds of times. The photographs arranged on the staircase walls are as familiar to me as my own family's gallery in our den. I take the steps two at a time like I have since second grade, when I first started coming here after school so Mom could take college classes.

I usually holler, "Tessa!" before I even reach the top step so she can swing open the door for me to make my leaping dive onto the middle of her bed. It's just one of those dorky things we do.

But I hold back this time. Like there's some shift in the atmosphere that I haven't put my finger on yet. In the past, I rarely called or sent a text to warn Tessa that I was coming over; I just showed up. And she never cared. She did the same thing to me. Just showed up.

It doesn't feel okay to do that today and I'm not sure why. It's like I'm not positive the same Tessa—the Tessa who would swing the door open so I could fly in—is on the other side of that door tonight. I'm unsure and a little sad about it.

But then again, maybe I'm totally wrong. I hope so.

When I arrive at the top of the staircase, with Tessa's door only a few feet away, the uncertainty holds me back. Tessa has no idea I'm here, and I'm going to feel dumb if she pops out to go to the bathroom or something and I'm standing there like I'm sneaking up on her.

Yeah, I have to be overthinking this.

"Tessa!" I call out.

I wait, like, thirty seconds, but it feels like thirty minutes. Nothing happens.

I don't hear any music coming from the room, so I'm not sure why she wouldn't have heard me.

"Tessa!" I belt out a little louder.

This time, the door creeps open, and Tessa's face pinches through the opening. Her eyes widen when she sees me, and she flings the door open wide.

"Alli? Whoa, what are you doing here?"

She just stands there with this semi-shocked expression on her face, and all the overthinking floods back in as a cold sweat comes over me. But then, Tessa breaks out into a big smile and throws her hands up. "You goon! You scared me half to death! Get in here."

I breathe a sigh of relief. Even though I don't make the traditional leap onto the bed, I'm in the room and plopped down on her beanbag chair before Tessa can say another word. She throws her cell phone on the bed and flops down on her belly next to it, facing me.

"Sorry I didn't call first . . . and for freaking you out," I say. "I yelled your name, but you didn't hear me. Were you sleeping or something?"

Tessa had been picking at a loose thread on her bedspread, her chin resting in the palm of her other hand. Her chin jerks up, and she gives me a dirty look. "*Sleeping*? When's the last time I took a nap after school, Alli? Really?" She reaches for her phone and looks down at it. "I was on the phone with someone. I was just hanging up when I heard you call my name."

"Oh, who were you talking to?"

It's always been natural for me and Tessa to be nosy about each other's business. And we rarely need to be prompted to tell everything we know and hear. School gossip, sibling problems, harassment from parents—we share it all. So, I'm kind of surprised when I notice Tessa stiffen after I ask her about the phone call. In fact, she would've normally already told me who she'd been talking to without me asking.

Then, it hits me.

"Tessa?" I squish to the edge of the beanbag chair and push closer to her bed. "Were you talking to a *guy*?"

No way! My best friend's into some guy, and she hasn't breathed a word! Whoa, is it Brent from her calculus class? Why wouldn't she tell me?

"No, I wasn't talking to a *guy*. You'd be the first to know." Tessa rolls off the bed and makes her way to the closet. The overhead light flicks on, and she pushes aside a few hangers. "Hey, do you still have my gray hoodie?" She calls out from the closet.

Wow. She shut that down fast, I think. *Why was she being so secretive, and would I really be the first to know if she was talking to a guy?*

"Yeah, it's in my drawer at home," I say. "I'll bring it over tomorrow." I stand and walk over to the bowl of chocolates

Tessa keeps on her dresser. I select a miniature Snickers bar and peel the wrapper off before joining her in the walk-in closet.

"So . . ." I'm not ready to let it go. *Obviously*.

"Who *were* you talking to?"

She pulls a cropped denim jacket off a hanger and brushes past me. "Shanice. We're getting together so she can show me a few routines." She pulls her shirt off, throws it on the bed next to the jacket, and pulls open the top dresser drawer. "She's picking me up in about forty minutes."

"You've been at practices every night this week! Don't you ever get a night off?"

Tucking a red tank top into her jeans, Tessa rolls her eyes. "I'm the new girl on the team, Alli. I have to work harder than the rest of them, okay?"

I sit on the edge of her bed while she pulls the denim jacket on. "I know, I get it. You feel like you have to learn all this new stuff and make an impression. But I don't understand why you have to hang out with these girls outside of practices and meetings." I sigh. "Seriously, Tessa. Why do you even want to be around them? You're nothing like them."

Tessa settles on the beanbag chair and adjusts her sandal strap. "I know, Alli. I'm sorry. I've been the worst friend. I know they're out of my league and that we don't have a lot in common, but I'm just trying to fit in and go with the flow. I hang out with them to show team loyalty and so they don't think I'm a snob or anything. Who knows? Maybe I can influence them for good."

It's my turn to roll my eyes. "Tessa, come on. You weren't even thinking about cheerleading three months ago. Your biggest stress was getting into AP Biology next semester and earning high enough grades to apply for college in the fall. And"—I have to say it—"you know you aren't going to influence *them*, Tessa. If anything, they're going to be a bad influence on *you*. Besides, you don't need them as friends." I stand up and throw my arms in the air. "You've got me!"

She swipes a pen from the nightstand and throws it at me. "Whatever, Alli. I just want to try something different before my high school years are over and I have to start adulting. Stop acting so possessive." She laughs. "I'll be fine."

"Yeah, right, you'll be fine. Just like you've been fine hanging out with them *every* night this week, and just like how you're hanging out with Shanice tonight instead of me. You didn't even call me! I had to show up on your doorstep and beg for your attention."

Tessa stands and grabs her purse. "Come on, drama queen. Let's go see if dinner is ready. My mom's making oven burritos."

"I can't. I'm supposed to head home soon."

Tessa yanks my cell phone out of my hand and holds it up to my face. "Call your mom and ask if you can stay for dinner. You know she won't care."

She doesn't have to tell me twice. "Well, since you mention *oven burritos*. How can I resist?"

I thumb to my mom's number and press the call button. Then, I put the phone to my ear as we head down the stairs and whisper to Tessa ahead of me, "So, did your parents end up paying for your cheer uniform?"

"Not yet. I'm still working on that."

Chapter Eight

MR. MARTIN PASSES BACK our science quizzes, carefully setting the papers facedown on the table in front of each one of us, like our future depends on what's written on the other side.

Knowing how awful I think I did, it's probably true. In that case, I'll be working at a fast-food joint until I'm sixty.

Just my luck that Tessa decided to be absent today, so there's no one to share my panicked look with. Not that Tessa, *Ms. Scholar* herself, ever has to worry about a test in science— or in any of her classes. She'll probably end up being valedictorian when we graduate in June, while I'll be lucky if I even graduate.

When Mr. Martin reaches our table, he slides my test down without a glance. When he gets to Brynne and Zach, he gives them both a smile. As I snatch my quiz up and go to shove it in my backpack without even looking at it, I notice Brynne's watching me.

"How'd you do?" she asks.

Rude, I think. *Is she trying to rub it in or what?* I push the test down into the backpack and hurry to zip it closed. "Don't know. I didn't look."

I'm sure she's really hoping I'll ask her the same thing, and I'm not about to give her that satisfaction. But instead, she pulls a pack of gum out of her sweatshirt pocket and holds it out to Zach and me. "Want a piece?"

Keeping an eye out for the teacher, Zach and I both reach for a piece. I unwrap mine and pop it in my mouth.

Strawberry flavor. Not my favorite.

Zach pulls out his science notebook and turns to a clean sheet, a pencil already primed and ready for taking notes in his hand. I've never seen somebody so eager to actually do *work* in class.

"Zach, seriously," I say. "I want to be just like you when I grow up." I point to his notebook.

He picks up the gum wrapper and studies it before folding it into a neat square, but I don't miss the flush in his cheeks and the tiniest hint of a smile that creeps over his face.

I kind of feel bad because I think he took that as a compliment when I was really being sarcastic. But I leave it at that.

"Where's Tessa today?" Brynne asks.

I look over at Brynne and shrug. "She sent me a text this morning saying she wasn't feeling well."

I plan to check on her after class. Tessa's never sick, so I was surprised when I saw her text before school this morning. She must be feeling awful.

That also means I have no one to eat lunch with. I wanted to ask Tessa how things are with her parents. I'd finally gotten out of her that the family meeting her parents had called with her and Aaron was to inform them that they were getting a divorce.

No wonder Tessa was so upset when I hadn't been there for her when she wanted to talk about it. Then, she kept it from me for a few weeks after that because her parents asked her and Aaron not to say anything to anyone. They said they wanted it to stay between the family for now. Naturally, Tessa couldn't keep it quiet for long, though—not from her best friend anyway.

This is all going through my mind when I hear Brynne ask me another question.

"Sorry, what?" I ask.

"Oh, I was asking if you want to eat lunch together. You know, since Tessa isn't here today."

I'm not sure how to answer. I don't really *know* Brynne, and I'm not even sure we have anything in common, but I guess it's not a big deal. At least I won't be sitting alone.

"Uh, sure. I have Mrs. Monroe for English Lit before lunch, and she usually finds some reason to keep us after the bell. Then, I gotta run and grab something from the snack bar," I say. "Where do you want to meet?"

She cringes. "Mrs. Monroe . . . *ugh*. My brother had her last year."

"Yeah, tell me about it."

"I brought a lunch, so I'll grab a table by auto shop. Meet you there?"

"Sure. Sounds good."

Mr. Martin cues up the Smart Board for today's lesson, so

we turn our attention to the front of the room. Without taking my eyes off the board, I reach for my notebook out of my backpack and think about hanging out with Brynne at lunch. I'm not sure if I'm dreading it or looking forward to it.

HANGING out with Brynne turns out to be really cool. She's always been low-key and quiet, so I never really went out of my way to talk to her. But she really opens up when we're alone.

While she nibbles on her sandwich and I wolf down nachos from the snack bar, Brynne tells me how she loves roller coasters and that she used to play the violin in middle school but has recently been wanting to take piano lessons. She mentions she has a brother who graduated from our school last year and who is now in his first year of college in Oregon. She took over his bedroom because it's bigger than hers but hates being the only kid left at home.

That's a ton of information to find out about someone in twenty minutes, especially from a classmate you thought was an introvert up to this point. But, like I said, Brynne really opens up over lunch.

The only new thing she learns about me is that I have no natural siblings but that my cousin, Avery, came to live with us when her mom, my Aunt Marg, passed away after a long battle with ovarian cancer.

Having lunch with Brynne wasn't too bad after all, and I'm glad that I didn't have to eat alone, but I worry about Tessa in the back of my mind. Her afternoons and most weekends are tied up with practices and games these days, so I feel like I have to compete with everyone just to hang out with her. I know her parents' divorce has got to be hard on her, but every time I ask Tessa if she wants to talk about it, she always seems distracted. Maybe she doesn't want to focus on the divorce or wants to avoid it altogether. Would I if it were my parents?

I miss sharing stuff with my best friend. We used to be able to talk for hours about everything and nothing at the same time and still be jazzed just to hang out together.

But I haven't hung out with Tessa outside of school for almost two weeks now. And even when we talk on the phone, she puts me on speaker so she can work on homework or clean her room because she gets home so late most nights and always has something to catch up on.

I sent Tessa a text before lunch (under the desk so Mrs. Monroe didn't catch me) to check on her, but she hasn't replied yet. I'm guessing she must be sleeping, which sounds amazing right now since Mr. O'Malley—we call him Mr. O for short—just assigned a twenty-question algebra assignment and told us to work on it independently for the rest of the class period. Which means I have forty more minutes of trying not to fall asleep.

The nachos from lunch sit like a lead pipe in my gut and I keep nodding off, even with my best attempt to stay awake. I pinch my wrist several times, but it doesn't help.

I'm about nine questions in and doing more doodling on my paper than solutions when I glance up and see Shanice, who sits two rows ahead of me, whispering to some girl whose name I can't think of right now but who I know is on the cheer team. While they talk, they keep looking back at me with smirks on their faces.

I'm wide awake now. And irritated.

What in the world is their problem?

I lean back slightly in my chair and flick the phone hidden in my lap to the front-facing camera so I can check to see if something's smeared on my face or if my hair's sticking up somewhere.

I don't see anything weird, so I push the phone back down in my lap and look up. The other girl is turned around and working on her math worksheet, but Shanice is twisted halfway in her seat and is staring at me, snapping her gum. She blows a big bubble, sucks it into her mouth, and throws me a dirty look before turning away.

I can't concentrate on the rest of the algebra problems while I sort through all the possibilities I can think of for why Shanice and her friend would be talking about me and throwing me dirty looks.

I decide that, when the bell rings, I'll confront Shanice and ask her what her problem is, but she's long gone before I can push past everyone trying to get out the single classroom door at the same time. I look for her in the hallway as long as I dare before I'm in danger of being late to economics.

Tessa finally answers my text when I'm in journalism, my last period of the day. I smile when I read her text.

Hey!! Sorry I didn't text back earlier. I slept allll afternoon. But my head feels better! Did ya miss me? Lol.

I browse through my phone emojis and choose the face with the rolling eyes before texting my answer: **Yeah, I guess**

you can say I missed ur sorry self today. I had to eat lunch with Brynne. Glad ur feeling better, slacker. Then, remembering that I wanted to ask her if she knew what Shanice's problem was, I add: **Can I stop by after school?**

Her reply is immediate.

Sure. Can you bring Starbucks?

I text back another eye roll emoji and then jam the phone in my hoodie pocket so I can finish typing up an article for the school newspaper.

One last chime comes through, and I lift the phone and see, **Thanks, bestie!**

I roll my eyes for real as I focus on the article again.

"You still owe me for the muffin the other morning," I mumble.

Chapter Nine

Our youth group is doing an outreach in the local community tonight.

Confession: I don't like helping with community outreach. It's not that I don't care about reaching out to people and inviting them to church. I just don't like putting myself out there and approaching complete strangers to do it. But here we are, handing out flyers to strangers and inviting the community to an upcoming youth rally our church is hosting next week.

Brother McGuire requires us to go out in teams of two for our safety. There are a couple girls in the youth group that I like to hang out with once in a while that probably would have teamed up with me, but I was in the bathroom when everyone picked partners.

You know what that means: I'm last and get stuck with whoever didn't get picked. So, my partner tonight is Kristin. Lucky me.

Predictably, she talks my ear off for the next thirty

minutes while we work the parking lot at a local pizza place. Not only am I starving from inhaling the scents of fresh pizza and chicken wings that hang in the air, but I'm also mentally exhausted from trying to keep my distance from Kristin. I keep sending her to the opposite side of the parking lot to work. But Kristin keeps insisting that we stay together and ends up wandering back over to my side every five minutes.

I'm ecstatic when we only have ten minutes left before we all meet up at the coffee shop across the street and call it a night.

I'm just wrapping up talking to a young couple that recently moved to Tucson to attend college, when I see Kim, Shanice, and a girl named Vanessa, who I also recognize from school, walk out the doors of the pizza place. I'm standing under a streetlamp, so I quickly sidestep into the shadows and hope they don't notice me.

Kristin jogs over to them and sticks a flyer out to Kim, who takes it and stares at it before passing it to Shanice. They talk to Kristin, but I can see the smug looks on their faces from where I stand.

I have no intention of making my presence known until they're long gone, but then Kristin looks right at me and yells, "Hey, Alli, do you know if they'll have a snack bar set up at the rally?"

All eyes turn to me.

I can't just stand in the dark in the middle of the parking lot and not look like a complete psycho, so I walk toward them, sending evil thoughts Kristin's way.

Kim's eyes widen when she recognizes me, and Shanice's smirk becomes an outright scowl.

"Oh, wow. It's . . . um, Alli, right?" Kim purrs like a content kitten. "You're Tessa's neighbor, aren't you?"

"No way, I totally know her," Vanessa says to Shanice, pointing at me.

"Yeah, I'm Alli." I keep my eyes on Kim, ignoring Vanessa and Shanice. "Tessa's my best friend." I don't know how Kim even knows Tessa and I live close to each other. I guess Tessa must've told her. Now I'm curious what other details Tessa's shared about me.

Shanice fans herself with the rally flyer. Kim reaches for it without taking her eyes off me, and Shanice hands it over.

Kim glances down at the paper, then back up at me. Then, she lifts the flyer up to my eye level like I've never seen the thing before now.

"Do you go to this church?"

Nah, we just found those flyers in a trash bin and decided to hand them out to random strangers, I want to say.

But before I can answer, Kristin jumps in. "Yes, our youth group is hosting the rally. You guys should come!"

I want to slap her for no real reason other than that she's making me look like—I don't know—a religious fanatic out here peddling church flyers. Which is sort of true, minus the *fanatic* part. I know I shouldn't feel this way, but, well, we're dealing with *Kim* and *Shanice,* popular cheerleaders with an insatiable need to make everyone else feel inferior. And with the ability to make life unbearable for me at school.

I shoot Kristin a silencing look. "Um, yeah, that's my

church," I say, my eyes dancing between the offensive flyer and Kim's equally offensive expression.

Kim's patronizing smile and honey-laced voice make my blood boil. "Oh, wow!" She says. "How cool is that? You two"—she looks between Kristin and me— "out here inviting people to a church meeting. How thoughtful of you."

I don't take it as a compliment, which is exactly Kim's intention.

Shanice and Vanessa stand there in their designer jeans and sandals with purses dangling on their arms that probably cost more than the root canal I had done last year. They stare at us while Kim bats her doe eyes at me.

Then, something predatory grows in Shanice's eyes as she fixes her glare on Kristin.

"So that means you wear"—Shanice twiddles her painted nails at Kristin's denim skirt— "and don't believe in wearing makeup or anything, right?" Her eyebrows raise as she turns to Vanessa. "I'm not even kidding, these guys live like *Little House on the Prairie*."

Vanessa busts out laughing.

Even Kristin chuckles and starts to say, "No, it's not like that—"

I move in close to Kristin. "Would you just shut up, Kristin?" I growl into her ear.

I'm seething. What a bunch of morons these girls are. For one thing, I'm wearing a super cute khaki jumper with a stylish, striped Forever 21 T-shirt under it and red Vans tennis shoes. That's a far cry from being barefoot and wearing a floral gunnysack dress that brushes the ground lest anyone *dare* see my ankles.

I have nothing to say to these losers and, at this point, I couldn't care less if they come to the youth rally or not. As a matter of fact, I hope they don't. The only reason they'd come, I'm sure, would be to mock it and gather more ammunition to use against me later.

I lock my hand onto Kristin's forearm and give a not-so-gentle tug while I plaster on my own fake smile as I look at the three snobs. I imagine raking my nails across their pretty faces.

"Well, we need to run. We're meeting up with our"—I almost say *youth group*— "friends. Catch you guys later." I keep my grip on Kristin, so she doesn't have a chance to say something else that'll make things worse than they already are.

She mostly complies but can't stop herself from throwing back one last appeal, "I hope you guys can make it!"

As we walk away, I quickly release Kristin's arm, so I don't look like I'm holding her captive. I can feel the other girls' icy stares burning right through my cute khaki jumper and piercing my chest. I want to cry, and I'm not even sure why. I think it has something to do with the whole "I don't like being different or the wrong puzzle piece" phobia I struggle with.

"Alli?"

I'm walking slightly ahead of Kristin now, having noticed that the streetlight is about to turn green, and I'm determined to make it across the street before I get stuck waiting for another cycle. All I want to do is make it to the coffee shop across the street and be out of sight of Kim, Shanice, and Vanessa.

Kristin calls out again, but I ignore her.

I'm halfway across the crosswalk when the light turns red. I pick up the pace.

Before I reach the corner, Kristin's at my side, slightly out of breath. "Alli, what's wrong? Are you mad?"

"No, I'm *not* mad," I spit out. "And nothing's wrong."

"Then why did you tell me to shut up back there? That was kind of rude."

When we make it to the sidewalk, I let out a long sigh, stop, and turn to her. "Sorry, Kristin. I shouldn't have told you to shut up. I really wanted to get out of there, and you kept going on and on."

We start walking again.

Kristin studies the ground as we head toward the bright lights of the coffee shop, but I notice her glance over at me. "What did I say?" she asks. "I was just answering their questions and—"

I spin and face her. "Don't you get it, Kristin? Those girls couldn't care less about a stupid youth rally. Didn't you see the look on their faces or hear what they were saying? They were messing with us." I shake my head and push ahead of her. I don't feel like getting into this right now.

Kristin doesn't push the issue, but I hear her mumble behind me just as we make it to the coffee shop doors.

"It's not a stupid youth rally, Alli."

Chapter Ten

I DON'T SEE Tessa until second period.

When I sent her a text before school, she said she had to be at the school early this morning to help with some posters for student council. She's not even on student council, so I don't know why she's helping with that. But I don't even bother asking Tessa about her comings and goings at this point because, more and more, they don't include me.

Tessa's backpack isn't at our table in science, so I figure she's running late.

I look at my watch. *Eh, she's got two minutes.* I toss my backpack on the table and rummage through it for extra lead since my mechanical pencil ran out last period. The small canister is empty.

I look around and notice Brynne and Zach digging out their stuff too.

"Hey, Brynne, do you have any lead?" I hold up my pencil for her.

"No," she shrugs. "Sorry. I've been meaning to buy some."

I don't bother to ask Zach because, for some out-there reason, he only uses the archaic #2 pencils most of us haven't used since elementary school.

Brynne glances behind her, then back to me. "Maybe Tessa has some?"

I glance over to where Brynne just turned from and see Tessa sitting at a far table . . . next to Shanice. Two guys share the table with them. And since Tessa's notebook is out in front of her already, it looks like she plans to stay there a while.

"What's she doing sitting over there?"

I look at Brynne as if she knows the answer, but I can tell by the look on her face that she's as clueless as I am.

On a regular day, I would have no problem marching over there and asking Tessa myself, but I won't do it with Shanice sitting there. After Friday night's run-in at the pizza place, she's the last person I want to draw attention from.

Pencil forgotten, I lower myself into my chair without taking my eyes off Tessa, sending vibes her way that are anything but pleasant. She must sense someone's staring because she glances my way and gives a little wave.

I throw my hands up in that universal gesture that can only be interpreted as, "What in the world are you doing?!"

Mr. Martin calls for everyone's attention at the front of the class, but my focus stays on Tessa. She pulls her phone out and taps out a text before pushing it back into her pocket and looking up front at the teacher. A moment later, I hear the *chirp* from my phone.

Mr. Martin is already into his lecture, but I stare down at Tessa's text.

Sorry. Was talking to Shanice and just ended up staying here. I'll catch u at lunch.

"Alli, do I need to confiscate that phone?" Mr. Martin—the whole class, in fact—is staring at me.

I shove the phone down in my backpack, my eyes never leaving Mr. Martin. "No, I'm done." I slink down in my seat.

"Well, I'm glad to hear that, but can you tell me why you have nothing out to take notes with?"

I'm ready to crawl under the table. My attempts at avoiding attention from Shanice are blown because I'm sure she's giving me every bit of her attention right now. She's probably enjoying my humiliation and wearing the smirk she always seems to sport when she looks at me.

I grab my notebook and another pencil—hopefully one with lead this time—out of my backpack and hope Mr. Martin and Shanice have both moved on. At this point, it doesn't even matter if my pencil has lead or not; I would fake it just so everyone would stop staring at me.

I DON'T HAVE to look for Tessa at lunch; she catches up to me just as I'm leaving my third period class.

"Hey, wait up!" she says.

I'm surprised to see her here since we always meet up at the tables outside. Besides, my English Lit class is on the opposite end of the school from the dance class she has before lunch.

"Hey, Tessa. What are you doing here? Aren't we meeting outside?"

Her face is a little flushed. I'm not sure if it's from dance or from running across campus. She stops right in front of me and tugs me over to the side of the hallway.

Looking at her straight on, I can tell her face isn't flushed from dancing or running.

She's mad.

"Alli, did you seriously try to convert Shanice and Kim to your faith the other night? Shanice showed me the flyer you gave her for some youth rally and said you and some other girl were walking around the parking lot trying to witness to people. That's just freaky, Alli."

I don't realize my mouth is hanging open until I'm ready to try to answer. I should've known Shanice and Kim would create some kind of drama out of nothing. And they did more than just stir up drama; they straight out lied.

"Oh, come on, Tessa, really? Kristin and I were just handing out flyers for an upcoming rally. In fact, it was Kristin who gave Kim the flyer. I walked up afterward. I never once invited any of them."

I'm sure my flushed face matches Tessa's right now. "Why would Shanice even tell you that? We didn't twist their arm or beg them to come. Why didn't she just toss the flyer in the trash if she wasn't interested? You know she's just trying to stir up drama, Tessa, and you're falling for it."

Tessa looks away, then back at me, her expression hard. "I doubt she's making the whole thing up. Why were you walking around parking lots harassing people, anyway?"

"*Harassing*? You're kidding, right? How were we *harassing* them by handing them a flyer?" I shove my hands on my hips and glare at her. "You do more *harassing* when you hawk those stupid candy grams on the front steps after school."

I don't want to discuss this with Tessa anymore, because the longer we talk, the more steamed I get.

She looks away again and doesn't bother to look back at me when she answers. "First off, the candy grams were a fundraiser for new equipment for the football team. That's not the point here, Alli. They think I'm hanging out with a religious freak who goes to a cult church that tells you how to dress and—"

"Stop, Tessa. Just stop. You've known me since elementary school. I've never been any different than what you see every day. And you *know* the church I go to because you've visited it before." I huff. "All of a sudden, your new snob friends think I'm weird, and you just go with it? Are you even listening to yourself right now? Do *you* feel this way about me too, or are you just following the mob, Tessa?"

It's as if I don't even know the Tessa who turns and looks me in the eyes and says, "Well, your religion never affected me before now, Alli. Sure, you've always dressed a little different from everyone, and people asked questions. But it wasn't a huge deal because, I don't know . . . you kept it to yourself, I guess. Now people aren't just *curious*; they're *offended* by your religion because you're sticking flyers in their face about it."

"*Offended*, Tessa? By what? What do you mean my *religion*? That doesn't even make sense. And, *again*, Kristin didn't stick the flyer in her face—"

Tessa throws a hand up. She doesn't want to hear it. Part of me wonders if she was just waiting for this excuse to shake me off as a dead weight so she could start a new identity with her posh friends. I no longer fit her ideal profile for a best friend, I guess.

She's already turned and has started walking away before I could even finish my sentence.

I let her walk away.

Because she no longer fits my ideal best friend profile either.

I SIT on the library steps during lunch, away from anyone I know who might see me. I don't bother to grab food from the snack bar, but just dig out a smashed protein bar I find in the bottom of my backpack. It tastes stale, but it doesn't matter.

I don't want to talk to anyone right now, but find myself mumbling to God anyway.

"I can't believe how Tessa's acting, God. I wasn't out beating people's doors down to come to church. She makes it sound like I was traipsing around Tucson, recruiting mindless people to join our cult and drink the Kool-Aid." I swallow back the lump that tries to creep into my throat and stare down at the mangled protein bar in my fist.

What bugs me the most is how Tessa said that no one's ever made a big deal of my faith—or *religion* as she referred to it— because I *kept it to myself*. Wow, that cut deep.

Have I been too quiet about my walk with God all this

time? As long as I didn't bring God up in conversation, everybody was cool with me doing my thing? Was that it?

I always answer honestly whenever someone asks me why I wear skirts and dresses and have long hair, but I don't go on and on about it. I tell them what I believe, and that's it. Was I slamming doors that I was supposed to be walking through instead?

The bell rings, and I scoop my backpack up from the step and run over to throw my mostly untouched bar in a nearby trash can. I already know I'm not going to make it across campus on time, but my feet fly to my next class, just in case. Thankfully, Mr. O'Malley doesn't make a big deal out of tardiness, because I make it in the door just after the bell rings.

I have to pass by Shanice's desk on my way to my seat. I hold my head up as I brush past but still hear her say, "Wow, you're sweating, Alli. Busy chasing imaginary demons around the campus during lunch?"

A chorus of laughs erupts around her, but I don't stop to even acknowledge her comment.

I hear several giggles and comments as I continue making my way to my seat. I can feel the tears clogging up my throat, but I don't dare let them near my eyes. Not in high school. I'd be eaten alive if anyone sees that Shanice's comment hit a raw nerve.

I've never felt so different. I've never stood out so much for who I am more than I do at this moment. If this is what being persecuted for your faith is like, I'm never gonna survive it.

After finally sliding onto my chair, I busy myself with pulling out my homework and grabbing one of the textbooks that have been left on our desks. I try to tune into the sounds of binder rings clicking open and closed and of papers and folders being shuffled around me while everyone else pulls out their own homework and gets ready for class.

If the crowd around Shanice is still snickering and staring at me, I'm unaware of it because I decide to tune it out, and I refuse to give my attention to anything near Shanice.

After everything with Tessa before lunch and then this, I feel like a hermit crab without his protective shell. Anything could crush me right now.

Chapter Eleven

"ALLI, CAN I COME IN?"

I don't bother answering because I know my mom will come in anyway. Besides, I don't trust my voice right now.

I know the door's opening because I hear the soft brushing of the wood against my carpet. My back is to the door, and I consider pretending I'm asleep. But before I can manage to close my eyes to try to pull it off, my mom peeks at me from the end of my bed.

"Honey, are you okay?"

I've been hearing that question a lot lately, and I always answer, "Yeah, I'm fine." But I'm not even going to lie right now since my face is probably blotchy, and I can feel that my eyes are swollen from crying. There's no way I could pull off another "I'm fine."

So instead, I do what I always do when I sense a mom-talk in the works: I scoot closer to the middle of the bed so she can sit down. That's the best answer I can give her right now.

Sitting on the edge of the bed, she reaches out and strokes my hair. Yeah, I'm seventeen, but I still can't resist another flood of tears when she does that. There's just something about a mom's touch that makes even an independent female on the brink of womanhood revert to a young girl again.

She lets me cry, never saying a word, her hand moving down my hair and then rubbing across my back. My mom can be relentless with her barrage of questions and nagging, but she also knows when to just let me have my space.

Eventually, she whispers, "It's going to be alright, Alli. Everything's going to be okay."

Right. How does she know that? She doesn't even know what's wrong with me. If I sat up right now and told her I was going to elope with a secret lover, I doubt she would still tell me, "Everything's going to be alright, Alli".

The thing is, she probably knows it's not anything as traumatic as that because I've never given her anything to be shocked about above taking a sip of my uncle's beer at a family reunion when I was twelve. And I only did that because my cousins dared me.

It almost irritates me that I'm so *predictable*. Everyone expects *good* old Alli to keep on being *good* old Alli.

The thought sobers me, and the fountain of tears shuts off as fast as it started.

Mom's hand stills on my back, but she keeps it there. "Do you want to talk about it?"

Suddenly, I do.

I sit up, and her hand drops from my back to her lap as she

watches me adjust myself against my pillow at the head of the bed. I fold my arms over my chest and pin her with my stare.

"Tessa has new friends in high places now, Mom. And I'm no longer suitable, I guess, to be her friend—much less her best friend." I huff. "And, to make things even better, according to Tessa, she and her friends think I'm a religious freak and don't want to be around me. In fact, her new friends are going out of their way to make me miserable about it."

The reality of everything makes the burden feel even heavier as I talk. I squirm against the pillows behind me.

"I don't walk around the school waving a Bible and acting like I'm better than anyone else. I just want to live my life and let other people live theirs. The last thing I was looking for was to be the center of attention, but that's exactly what I got for doing *nothing*." I stare right at my mom, making sure she's getting this. "I seriously didn't do *anything* to deserve this. So, tell me, Mom, how you can say that everything's going to be alright?"

I expect to see pity—maybe even anger—at my outburst, but her expression remains blank, like she's waiting for the end of the story to come. Maybe she's just waiting for the storm of my frustrations to pass because she knows that saying anything right now would be pointless.

I realize how confrontational my glare is and lower my eyes to the throw pillow bunched up on my lap.

Mom sighs deeply, and I almost feel bad. I didn't really mean to bite her head off, and to be honest, I'm kind of embarrassed that I dumped all that on her. I'm not fourteen anymore.

I should be able to handle a little immaturity from my peers at school.

And normally, it probably wouldn't bother me all that much. It's not like I've never been teased or bullied before. But I've never been bullied about my faith. And I've never lost a best friend over it either. Both are uncharted territories for me, and I realize I don't know how to handle either one.

I peek up at my mom and find that she's still looking at me with those vibrant green eyes I'd always wished I'd inherited but didn't, and I know she sees through my parchment-paper facade to the broken pieces of my heart. She's replaced her blank expression with a look of compassion. I'm not sure which I prefer right now.

My mom's always ready with just the right thing to say to encourage me and smooth down my ruffled feathers. I mentally prepare myself for the launch into one of her counseling sessions, where I sit and listen to the soothing sound of her voice bringing me back to reality and making me feel better.

Instead, she reaches for my hand, dips her head to catch my eye, and says, "I'm sorry, Alli. This must be very painful for you."

I don't know why her words make me feel cheated. I mean, what did I expect her to say? Did I unleash my troubles on her, hoping she would have the magic words to make it all better?

Maybe I thought she'd offer to pray down angels from Heaven, and, miraculously, Tessa would call before the night was over and beg for forgiveness.

But life rarely works out that way, and that makes me feel worse. Tessa probably *won't* call tonight, I'll still get dirty looks and snide comments from the snob squad, and my lunch hour will probably be spent hiding outside the library for the rest of my high school career.

"Would you like me to pray with you, honey?" Mom asks. "I don't have the answer, but I know God does."

It's my turn to sigh, but at least her offer to pray came through. I nod. "Yeah, I think so."

I'm going to need all the prayers I can get this week.

WE HAVE A VISITING evangelist at church this morning.

He's a fireball and really preaches the house down. He's also super cute and single, which makes all the single girls on the front row pews sit up straighter and pay attention. You've never seen a pew full of young ladies turn so spiritual all of a sudden.

I might've stood and clapped a little extra too if he weren't almost nine years older than me. *Too old.*

The evangelist really runs home how we're to be a light shining bold and bright for all the world to see and how we should never be ashamed of who we are but should be right-eously proud to be called a Christian.

He hits so many points of what I've been struggling with lately that I almost turn in my pew to search my mom's face for traces of guilt. It's like this preacher was reading my mail.

Of course, I know my mom wouldn't have shared my dirty laundry with a visiting minister none of us know, but it creeps me out that he knows exactly how I've been feeling.

The only other logical explanation is that God's trying to speak to me. I don't really feel confident about that either, because I haven't been the best company for him lately. In fact, for as often as I've talked with him recently, I wouldn't be surprised if I went to pray one night and God said, "I'm sorry, but who are you again?"

"The Bible says in Matthew, chapter five, that God calls us to be a light to this world," the preacher says, stepping away from the pulpit and making his way off the platform. Instantly, two rows of teenage girls transform into model saints as they back him with a chorus of amens.

"Men don't light a candle, then hide it under something," he continues, pacing slowly in front of the platform as he connects with the congregation.

"No. We put that candle on the highest surface so the light can reach every possible dark place. That's what God expects of us, church. Verse sixteen says, 'Let your light so shine before men, that they may see your good works, and glorify your Father which is in Heaven.' A *light* in contrast to the darkness of the world."

The preacher stops near my seat, and I hold my breath, hoping to stay off his radar.

"God wasn't merely making a suggestion," he continues, moving past me.

I take a deep breath.

"He was issuing a commandment to share—not hoard—your light and your testimony with a lost world."

I really try to take it all in and find myself nodding in agreement as he speaks to us, but something about how he points out that we should let our light shine before others and that they would, in turn, glorify God doesn't sit right with me. I'm not questioning God straight out, but I can't help but wonder how sharing my light in that parking lot (Okay, Kristin was the one who *really* did the sharing, but I was part of it by default) backfired on me.

Instead of Kim, Shanice, and Vanessa being inspired and drawn in by what we tried to share and God receiving glory from it, they did the opposite and threw it back in my face.

Mom hasn't brought up my meltdown since the night she prayed with me, but I've noticed her worried stares when she thinks I'm not looking.

I wonder if she mentioned anything to my dad, but I doubt it. He would've already insisted we sit down and talk it out. Out of the two of them, Dad's the talker and Mom's the worrier.

I think I take after my mom because I'm stressing over going to school tomorrow. I'm dreading getting the silent treatment from Tessa and having to sit by myself before school and during lunch. It's not like I don't have lots of friends I talk to in my classes; I've just never *hung out* with any of them. It's always been me and Tessa, and I guess I never felt like I needed anyone else.

Do I really need anyone else?

The youth all sit in the first few rows of pews for service, and I see the back of Kristin's head three girls down in the row in front of me. She's avoided me ever since I went off on her after outreach that night.

The youth rally turned out to be a lot of fun, but I spent

most of the night watching the door, praying that Shanice, Kim, and Vanessa didn't show up just to cause trouble or to check out what kind of church I attend.

Being Apostolic, we're expressive and demonstrative in our worship, which includes jumping, shouting, and getting loud. The Bible says to make a joyful noise, and we take that seriously.

But I didn't want Kim and Shanice witnessing any of that. My stomach did flops all night as I imagined them seeing a service with that kind of worship and whipping out their phones to record it to show everyone at school.

The evangelist invites everyone to gather around the front, breaking me out of my inner thoughts, so I stand and make my way to spend a few minutes in prayer. I find a vacant place at the far end of the platform behind the piano, where there are lots of dark shadows and where no one will really notice me.

I kneel and tuck my face into the crook of my arm. My mind races like a hamster on a wheel as I think about the craziness of the past few weeks and about what the next weeks hold for me. I'm already exhausted trying to think of creative ways to avoid Tessa and her crowd at school.

I'm going through the motions of talking to God with whatever random words come to my lips when I feel a hand rest on my back and hear a small voice next to me begin to pray.

With my forehead now resting on my clasped hands, I open one eye to see who dares invade my private space. I spy a blue sleeve with a ribbon sewn around the cuff.

Kristin. I should have known.

I rub my eyes and reach for a tissue from a nearby box,

making it clear that I'm done praying. I glance over at Kristin and feign a look of gratefulness. "Thanks for praying with me, Kristin," I say as I push myself up to a standing position, leaving Kristin still kneeling.

She looks up at me and smiles. "Of course, Alli. I know you've been going through something." She stands and gives me a quick hug. "I'm here if you ever need to talk."

I nod. Her words actually touch me because I see the sincerity on her face. "Thanks. That means a lot."

And, I must admit . . . it does.

Chapter Twelve

BRYNNE, Zach, and I work through a reaction rate experiment that involves using Alka-Seltzer tablets in water. Zach's in charge of keeping detailed records as we work through changing the variables, like pressure and temperature.

We end up throwing the Alka-Seltzer tablets at each other and poking fun at Zach's tiny handwriting.

It's a blast working with the two of them, especially when Brynne accidentally knocks over the glass of water for our experiment, and we watch Zach scramble in a panic to grab the notes and worksheets scattered all over the table.

The fifty minutes of class go by in a blur and, even though I placed myself with my back to Tessa so I can't see her, I don't think even once about her sitting with Shanice on the other side of the room. But after we clean up and put away our supplies, the knots in my stomach tighten up again as I wait for the bell to ring.

When it finally does, I linger. I can't explain why. Even

Zach gives me an odd look when he notices. I guess I don't want to take the chance of accidentally running into Tessa going out the door or out in the hallway, especially with Shanice glued to her side.

Zach nods at me as he hurries past. "See you tomorrow, Alli."

I wait until everyone has left and I'm sure I won't run into Tessa, then make it to my English Lit class just as the bell rings.

I know I have it coming.

Mrs. Monroe is in true form as she screeches at everyone to find our seats, get our daily journals out, and start on the writing prompt she's written neatly on the whiteboard. Before I can creep past the extinct pencil sharpener screwed into the counter just inside the door, she's already barked out four or five student names, and it isn't because she's taking attendance.

Her radar must've been on hyperdrive, because her head whips around, and she catches me red-handed, guilty face and all. Even though the bell only rang ten seconds ago, it feels like an hour. *I'm busted.*

"Ms. Mancini, *where* have you been?" Her eyes blink rapidly as her lips curl together into a tight mass the size of a small jawbreaker.

Why do old people insist on calling us by our last names when we're in trouble?

"Sorry, Mrs. Monroe. I got caught up doing something," I lie.

Most of the time, I'd get one more quick tongue-lashing, or she'd write my name on the board for detention in black marker with her bold cursive writing and then move on, but today she's not having it.

She still writes my name on the board, but instead of saying something snappy as I shuffle humbly to my seat and then focusing her attention back on the class, she doesn't move. She stands there, glaring at me over the top of her wire glasses.

"Come here, Ms. Mancini."

I turn slowly, knowing I'm about to bear the brunt of all the anger and frustration she's feeling with the class right now. I bite down hard on my bottom lip and make my way to her desk, training my eyes on the fists pressed against her hips instead of daring to look her in the face. The last thing I want her to see is my defiance right now because it'll only get her more riled up.

When I reach her desk, I tuck my hands under the shoulder straps of my backpack, heave a big sigh, and grit my teeth.

"Why were you late?" she asks.

Didn't she already ask me this? Is this a trick question?

I want to come back with a snarky, "Actually, my big toe was inside the door before the bell rang, so I'm not actually late," but I manage to keep it tame.

"I told you. I had to take care of something."

The rest of the class is oddly quiet. I'm so glad my scolding is providing the entertainment for this hour. I feel the heat creep up my neck and settle on my cheeks. I'm somewhat relieved that I'm facing Mrs. Monroe instead of the students so I don't have to view what I'm sure is a sea of amused expressions.

"You had to . . . take care of something. Is that right? Why don't you share with all of us what was so important that you couldn't make it to class on time? Is your time more valuable than that of the rest of your peers who were able to show up on time?"

Her voice is worse than chalk scraping across a board, and I find myself wanting nothing more than to snatch a handful of tissues from the box on her desk and shove them down her throat.

I've never been so angry and humiliated. The rage burns in my gut, bubbling into my chest cavity. I know if it makes it to my mouth, fire's going to come exploding out and burn Mrs. Monroe to a crisp. But I don't care what happens at this point as long as she gets off my case.

I don't even try to hide the defiance on my face as I lift my chin to meet her eyes. "Why don't you leave me alone and stop harassing me?" My voice is low but not so low that the students sitting at the front of the room can't hear. "Half the kids in this class are late all the time, and you never make them tell you what they were doing or rail on them in front of everyone."

My knees quake. I don't recognize my own voice as I unleash the hurricane of my frustration out on her. I feel justi-fied because she's the one who started it.

"Maybe I was in the bathroom throwing up or something. Or maybe I wanted to finish my cigarette before I came in."

That last comment makes me wince because I know I've gone over an invisible line. I can see it in her face. Mrs. Monroe doesn't look mad anymore; she looks as shocked as I am.

We stand there staring at each other for a moment, which

feels like an eternity, before the salty sting washes into my eyes and I have to look down.

You could've heard a pin drop in the room. Right now, I wouldn't mind too much if a bomb dropped and took us all out just to end this horrible standoff.

"Alli, please wait for me in the hall," Mrs. Monroe says, her voice as tragic as when we read the play *Macbeth* out loud in class last semester.

For a moment, I'm afraid my knees will buckle, and I'll drop right here in front of everyone, but I manage to turn back toward the door and make my way out to the hall, even lifting my chin in an attempt to look like that whole scene didn't just age me ten years.

A sticky trickle slides down my back as I wait in the hall. The faint scent of pine and bleach drifts over from a nearby supply closet. The bright sun streaming through the window next to me illuminates a portal of dust particles that dance across my vision as I blink back the tears.

What I wouldn't give to hop onto that dust portal and be transported to another world where cheerleaders, nosy teachers, and ex-best friends don't exist. But when I hear the click of the door latch releasing behind me, there's no doubt I'm still living in reality.

I turn to face Mrs. Monroe. There's no fight left in me as I keep my eyes trained on her brown, leather loafers with her skin-colored liners peeking out the tops.

Since she's allowed the door to close behind her, I assume she must've opened the one that's between the classroom and Mr. Conrad's next door so he can keep an eye on the class. I also assume that my hope that she'll make this quick isn't going to happen. I might as well get my part over with.

"Sorry, Mrs. Monroe. I guess I've had a bad day—a bad week, honestly. I really am sorry."

She's close enough that I can almost feel the exhale of her breath. "No, Alli. I actually owe *you* an apology. There are several students who would've deserved my public scolding. *You* are not one of those students."

My head jerks up, and we lock eyes. My lower lip begins to tremble, but there's no way I can get all emotional out here in the hallway, especially with a cute guy from my first period stepping out of a class across the hall and heading our way.

Mrs. Monroe gives me a tender smile. "I guess I had a bad day too."

I nod my head like it's no big deal until the guy passes, then I let my shoulders and pride deflate. "Thank you for understanding. I won't be late again." I try to smile back at her, but I can't quite manage it. I'm still trying to keep my emotions in check, and any wrong move might make them slip.

"Do you want to talk about it? The Alli I just witnessed in that room wasn't the student I usually see walk into my class every day. Are you okay?"

For a moment, her sincere concern and motherly tone break my defenses down and almost make me feel like pouring out my troubles. But what I'm feeling would take a whole lot longer than five minutes standing in a high school hallway.

I shrug. "No, it's okay, Mrs. Monroe. Like I said, I've had a tough week, but I'll get through it. Sorry. It won't happen again."

Her brief touch on my shoulder is oddly soothing and brings back memories of Nonna Mancini's warm hugs that always made my burdens feel just a little bit lighter.

As we turn to make our way back into the class, I try to adjust my expression and roll my eyes, so I appear to look like I'd just endured a boring lecture from an angry Mrs. Monroe instead of the apology and compassion I wasn't expecting in a million years.

It's the best I can do to try to salvage my pride in front of my peers.

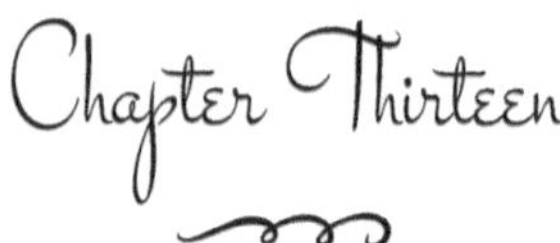

Chapter Thirteen

"*Chad Barton?* Are you *serious?* How'd you get an interview with him?"

Maribel, a classmate in my journalism class, is standing so close that her floral body spray makes me gag.

She's usually chill and keeps to her group of friends, but when she heard I'm interviewing Chad Barton—one of the heartthrobs on the football team—she was all over it.

Am I the only one seeing this? I wonder. I mean, she's acting like I ousted her from a spot on the Olympic swim team and crushed her lifelong dream.

"I don't know, Maribel." I throw my hands up. "Ask Mr. Porter. He's the one who told me to interview Chad."

"You're not even on the athletic team. I thought you only do the academic stuff."

I don't have time for this. I need to find one of our loaner cameras so I can get going. "Again, ask Mr. Porter, Maribel. Maybe it's because Scott's absent today." I move past her. "Besides, you're not in athletics either, so why do you care?"

Maribel's already making her way to Mr. Porter's office before I make it halfway across the room. I glance over at her team, who design the layout for our school newspaper and yearbook. They're deep in discussion and don't even seem to notice that Maribel is missing. I'm not surprised.

They know how she is. Maribel's dramatic about everything.

I shrug and head toward the equipment room. *Maybe I should just let her have the assignment. Everyone knows Maribel's had a crush on Chad since our sophomore year.* It's a long walk to the locker room on the other side of the campus, and I'll probably have to wait in the hot sun forever until Chad comes out anyway.

It briefly crosses my mind to follow Maribel into Mr. Porter's office, but I must admit, it's a matter of principle now. Besides, she has nothing to worry about. Chad Barton *is* one of the hottest guys on the football team, so he wouldn't notice me even if I waltzed around campus wearing a clown costume.

I lift a Nikon D3500 camera from the hook on the wall and grab my notebook from my backpack, mentally running through some of the questions I copied down to ask Chad. I wonder if I can throw in one or two that aren't football related like, "What do you think about girls who are simpler, kind of like the 'girl next door' type?" Or, "Don't you think cheerleaders are such a bore?"

Yeah, like I would really do that. Although I *am* just the tiniest bit curious about what his answers would be.

Either way, by the time I'm halfway to the locker room, I'm smiling. Why wouldn't I be? I'm interviewing Chad Barton.

~

I'M on my third question and doing way more writing than Chad's speaking. I'm writing random stuff just to be, well, doing *something* to keep my nerves in check.

I'm pretty sure it has something to do with the fact that Chad's been looking right at me the whole four and a half minutes (not that I'm keeping time) of our interview.

I don't know. I guess I thought he'd be super distracted talking to a nobody like me—anxious to get back to his locker room buddies, browse through all the likes on his social media posts, and get on with his day. But I'm surprised how super laid-back Chad is and how he really thinks about his answers to my interview questions. Maybe all high school celebrities are just used to the attention.

I stare down at the next question written in my notebook. It's obvious that I copied these from the internet and that I didn't have time to read through them before Maribel got in my face. And besides, try talking to a gorgeous guy while trying to keep your head in the game.

"So, um . . . yeah," I say. "How do you think your coaches and teammates would describe you?"

Lifting my chin, I give Chad my brightest smile, trying to act like this private interview isn't affecting me at all, which is the furthest thing from the truth.

Chad smiles back, and I can't help but notice the adorable

little indents at the sides of his cheeks. One dark ringlet from his mop of unruly curls hangs over one eye, and I can see the shadow above his upper lip where a layer of sweat has gathered.

I look back down at my notebook. *Anywhere* but Chad.

"Hmm, that's a tough question, uh, what's your name again?" he asks.

I have no problem giving Chad my full attention at this point. I can't believe he asked for my name. *He wants to know my name!*

"Alli." That's the best I can squeak out. I almost make the mistake of asking the standard, "And yours?" when I'm the one that came out here to interview *him*. Oh, dear lord, I would've *died*.

"Oh, cool . . . Alli. Got it. Thanks. So, I'm almost positive my teammates would say I can be motivating and that I have a team-spirit attitude, on and off the field. I think the coaches would feel like that too. I'm all about the team, and I'm really dedicated to succeeding." He raises his eyebrow at me. "Are you quoting me on this?"

His laugh is like a river current washing over me. I know I shouldn't step into the middle of those waters, but the current drags me in.

I laugh and bat my eyes over the top of my notebook, ignoring the tug on my conscience—the warning in my spirit. *I got this. This isn't going anywhere*, I tell myself.

A couple football players come jogging out of a side door and head out to the field, and the magic is broken.

"Let's go, Barton," one of the guys calls out.

Chad waves, then looks back at me. "Gotta go. See you around, Alli."

I'm still grinning like a dork. Then, I realize I didn't even write his last answer down. I also haven't taken a photo for the article yet.

"Oh, wait, hang on. Real quick." I shove my pencil into the spirals of my notebook and set the notebook on the ground. Lifting the camera to my face, I ask him to pose for a quick shot.

Chad flicks the stray curl back into place, straightens, and smiles right into the camera—dimples and all—and I seriously think about emailing myself a copy of the photo later, imagining he's smiling just for me.

Yeah, right, I think. *Who am I kidding? Chad Barton won't remember even speaking to me after today.*

But he *did* ask me my name!

Chapter Fourteen

Best friends are overrated.

I convince myself that I don't need Tessa. That I'm done with her.

I have lots of friends in my youth group at church who I hang out with on occasion, and I usually get along just fine with kids at school, but I never saw the need to have more than Tessa.

We were both eight when Tessa moved to Tucson, Arizona, and into my neighborhood. Our moms met at a PTO meeting at our school. My mom was the room mother for my second-grade class and asked if Tessa could sit by me on her first day of school so she wouldn't feel all alone.

I took the responsibility seriously—sharing my colored pencils, giving her a tour of the playground at recess, and giggling with her behind our folders during class. By the end of the first week, we were best friends.

Kids don't need to swim through a bunch of drama to

make friends. They just bump shoulders with the right some-one, ask them if they want to be friends, and it's a done deal.

Back when we were younger, the fact that Tessa and her family didn't attend church or believe the way my family did wasn't a big deal. In elementary school, we didn't have deep theological discussions about God and faith. And the rare times God came up between Tessa and me, she would always say, "Oh, yeah, I believe in God too," and that was enough to keep us happy with the way things were.

As we got older, the crevice between us widened into a gap, but it was never big enough that we couldn't build a bridge to meet in the middle. After a while, we just stopped talking about it.

If we didn't talk about church, God, the existence of a heaven or hell, or anything else faith-related, then . . . well, there was nothing to disagree about. Our friendship remained safely intact.

Even in middle school, when our outward differences became more obvious as we became more sensitive about our appearances and then the opposite sex, and as other people drew attention to my skirts and long hair, Tessa always brushed it off with nothing more than a shrug, as if to say, "So my friend's a little quirky. So what?"

More serious questions were unavoidable when we entered our high school years. I started thinking more seriously about making my own choices about my faith instead of just going along with what I'd always been taught by my parents. My walk with God became intentional instead of just obligatory.

Suddenly, I wasn't just going along with Tessa's crazy ideas of sneaking out to each other's houses in the middle of the night, skipping class, and hiding in the student bathroom without expressing guilt or outright refusing to do it. We were still best friends and were closer than sisters in most everything, but there was an impending storm on the horizon that both of us saw coming but chose to ignore.

The problem is really with me. It's simple: Tessa never professed to be anyone different, while I did. That makes me the one living the lie.

And Tessa was the one to expose it.

So, I'm back to square one. Like I was back in second grade —the pre-Tessa, pre-best friend era. I have no choice but to discover a new normal, one without Tessa in my life.

It's time to face the fact that we've always had a fracture in our relationship and that now, that fracture has finally crumbled our friendship and set us on different paths. It's time to put on my brave-girl face when I look in the mirror every morning and remind myself: *I don't need Tessa.*

Chapter Fifteen

Brother McGuire is talking to Anthony when I walk into youth class. The conversation looks serious, so I start tiptoeing backward out of the room.

I don't think they've seen me come in, but then I hear Brother McGuire call out, "You can come in, Alli!"

"It's okay," I say. "I'm a few minutes early anyway. I'll come back."

But Anthony stops me this time. "Hey, Alli, you're just the person I wanted to see." He weaves his way through the folding chairs that are set up in neat rows across the room, slips his Bible onto a chair at the end of the third row, and glides up to me.

"What's up?" I ask.

"I was wondering if you would help me out with something."

Anthony's one of those super dudes every youth group has.

You know, the kind of guy who gets along with everyone, has a ridiculous number of talents, is good-looking and charming, and is way too spiritual for the rest of us mortals.

It's not that he walks around with a better-than-thou attitude. Not at all. Anthony just has his act together and is serious about his faith. He doesn't have to flaunt it; it just shows in how he carries himself.

I've always thought of our youth leader, Brother McGuire, as a kind of Moses figurehead and of Anthony as his Joshua that he's preparing to take over for him as youth leader someday. The youth group sits in awe when Anthony leads our services because his passion for God just oozes out of him. So having him ask me to help with something is pretty humbling.

"Sure," I say. "What do you need?"

"Well, Brother McGuire wants me to form a youth committee to plan out next quarter's activities for the youth department. You were one of the first people who came to mind. Would you be willing to be a part of the committee?"

I'll admit, I'm flattered, and I kind of need the self-esteem boost right now, so I'm all for it. "Yeah! That would be great. I'd love to help. When do we meet?"

Several others have come in while we talk and are starting to get seated. Class will be starting soon.

Anthony looks around and then turns back to me. "I'll get with you on Sunday. The first meeting will probably be next week sometime. I need to get with a few other people. Do you have any suggestions of anyone else who'd be a good fit for the committee?"

A couple names jumble about in my mind, but no one stands out until Kristin walks through the door. Kristin gets on my nerves for some reason, but she has a kind heart and really loves God. I'm sure I'll regret it, but I think I'm doing the right thing.

"Actually," I point over to where Kristin sits, digging through her purse, "I think Kristin would be a good choice."

Anthony follows my finger and nods. "Great idea!" He smiles. "Thanks, Alli. I'll talk to her after class." He turns and heads to the front of the room to get things started.

Scanning the back row of chairs, I only spy an empty seat in the middle, close to Kristin. Which means I'll have to clamor over everyone's legs to reach it. I groan and make my way over. I might've just vouched for Kristin, but that doesn't mean I want to sit near her or be forced to talk to her right now.

But the back row gives me the chance for a quick exit when class is over, so I make my way over. The youth usually get together after class to meet up at a fast-food place and hang out for an hour or two. Normally, it's something I look forward to, but I'm not feeling it tonight, so a quick exit is what I'm shooting for.

I'm sure I'll get several texts later from the other youth asking where I am and if I'm coming. I'll just make up some excuse about having homework to catch up on or something. It's better than telling them that I'm mad at the world right now and that I'm not the greatest company. The last thing I need is for my phone to blow up with "praying for you" and "you wanna talk?" messages.

I don't want that kind of attention. What I want right now is to go back to being in the background instead of feeling like I'm standing in the center of a war zone, dodging bullets. I just want to go back to being boring, wallflower Alli instead of bearing the labels of Tessa's ex-best friend, religious freak, and psycho-girl-in-English Lit that I've unwillingly taken on recently.

"Nice job on your interview with Chad Barton, Alli."

I don't even realize Mr. Porter's talking to me until everyone at the table looks my way.

"I know I kind of threw it on you at the last minute," he continues.

The journalism team sits around an ancient, wood table that Mr. Porter inherited from the woodshop department eons ago. It's enormous and several inches thick (it must've taken the whole football team to move over here) and filled with carved names that Mr. Porter has stopped bothering trying to sand off.

The table is the focal piece of the room, which really used to be a teacher's lounge back in the '80s, and is our beloved journalism mascot where we hold our weekly Friday meetings and that we use for spreading out equipment, papers, and photos for our yearbook and newspaper layouts.

I sit at the opposite end of the table from Mr. Porter, so I have a clear view of everyone staring at me. Maribel's the only one not sending an encouraging smile my way, and I know it's because she still resents the fact that I got to interview Chad instead of her.

I can't resist gloating in the moment. "Thanks, guys."

Mr. Porter calls everyone's attention back as he goes over next week's assignments.

"So, listen up. Scott couldn't be here today. He's covering a feature on the Mock Trial Championship in Phoenix that some of our juniors are involved in." He taps the paper in front of him. "You can see on the agenda that he's requested some opinion pieces for next month's issue. Any ideas?"

Opinions are one thing high school journalists never run out of, and several hands shoot up right away. Maribel's practically popping in her seat.

Mr. Porter nods her way. "Maribel?"

Maribel lifts herself from one of the low stuffed chairs someone dragged over from the conference room next door. She's barely five feet tall and, sitting down, Maribel's chin is only inches above our massive mascot table, so it's not hard to forget she's there.

Until, that is, she starts talking and her shoulder-length black curls bounce in cadence with the staccato stop-and-go of her annoying voice. I stare at the back of her head and imagine a toy poodle begging at the dinner table.

"I think we should do an opinion piece on how the school dress code is outdated. I'm not kidding; I don't think the policy has been updated since the '50s," she says, smacking her lips every couple of words.

I roll my eyes, because it never fails that someone will challenge the school dress code every few months and not one thing has ever come of it.

Mr. Porter's diplomatic, as usual. "Tell you what, Maribel. Write up a piece, and Scott and I will look it over."

With a satisfied toss of her curls, Maribel flounces back in her seat and starts scribbling in a notebook perched on her lap.

Mr. Porter calls on a couple more students, but I tune them out because a few unrelated ideas pop into my head that I want to share with the youth committee this weekend, and I need to write them down before I forget. I flip my notebook open to an empty page and start jotting them down.

When Luke, who sits next to me, jabs me hard with his elbow, I throw him a dirty look. "What, Luke?"

He throws a look back at me and jerks his head toward the other end of the table. "Porter's talking to you," he hisses.

My head spins back to Mr. Porter, who stands holding a paper in his hand and looking at me over the rim of his glasses.

"Oh, sorry, Mr. Porter. What was that?"

He snaps the paper once and looks down at it. "I was asking if you have an idea for an opinion piece."

After his praise for my successful piece on Chad Barton, I feel obligated to keep up the momentum. I frantically try to come up with some kind of a half-decent idea.

"Um, what about a piece on the consequences of risk-taking behavior in teenagers?" I just throw it out there, making my contribution, but hoping Mr. Porter will shrug it off and move on to the next person.

Instead, he sets the paper down on the table, pulls the pencil from behind his ear, and scribbles down my suggestion.

"Not a bad idea, Alli. I'll jot it down and see what Scott thinks."

Ugh, I hope Scott shoots it down. The topic is so cliché and has to be one of the most mundane things to write about. There's no way Scott's going to think that writing about the risks teenagers take and the consequences of those risks is newsworthy.

At least, that's what I *hope* Scott thinks.

Chapter Sixteen

"I DON'T KNOW what you have against me, Alli. I just want to be your friend."

I should've known it would happen sooner or later, but I'm still surprised when Kristin runs up behind me in the church parking lot when I go to grab my jacket from the car. I wonder how long she's been spying and waiting to catch me alone. I guess I should be glad it's Kristin and not a serial killer because, otherwise, I'd be in a bad place right now.

I stall her off while I work the zipper up on my jacket, which shouldn't take nearly as much time as I drag it out to take. I'm trying to decide just what it is about Kristin that makes me keep pushing her away.

Zipper finally in place, I have no other distractions to keep me from answering, so I say the first thing that pops into my head: "I don't really think it's you, Kristin."

The realization hits me at the same time the words come

rolling off my tongue, as if they'd been waiting on the sidelines the whole time. "I think it's me."

Kristin tilts her head and gives me a puzzled look.

I continue. "Maybe I feel convicted when I get around you. Like you're the polar opposite of my walk with God right now and seem to be doing everything right, while I seem to be doing everything wrong." I grin, attempting to loosen the tension I've created with my grand confession.

"When I get around you, I feel like I should be doing better than I am. But I guess that's what we *should* be for each other —someone who influences the other to be a better version of themself. A challenge. An inspiration."

Kristin smiles but looks like she's still only getting half of what I'm trying to say.

Sheesh, I'm just digging a bigger hole here.

"It's supposed to be a good thing, Kristin," I say. "Stop looking like you just caught me reading all your private journals or something. You're freaking me out."

We both laugh.

Then, she does something that *really* freaks me out. She hugs me.

When she steps back, I see her eyes are bright with tears. I hope she doesn't get all emotional on me because I'm not prepared for that at all.

"It's crazy, Alli, but I've actually always thought that way about *you*," she says.

I know the shock on my face is obvious. "I don't see how—"

"You just always seem so put together and confident, and,

well, I'm not. I'm awkward and never know what to say or I end up saying too much. You always have the right words for everything, which is obvious since you write for your school newspaper, and I've seen some of the material you've written for the church plays and stuff."

Kristin reaches up and tucks a loose strand of hair behind her ear and smiles timidly. "I've always admired you—even wanted to be like you. Now here you are telling me that I make you feel less when you're around me. I think we have a lot to learn from each other."

Kristin and I stand in silence, digesting our conversation.

I think we're both content that we've said everything we wanted to say, but Kristin proves me wrong. "Do you want to be prayer partners? Maybe we can be an encouragement to each other."

I start to chuckle until I look at her face and see she's serious. "Prayer partners?"

Eyebrows raised, she gives me a friendly scolding. "Yes, Alli. *Prayer partners.* You *do* know what those are, right?"

"Yes . . . I do. But to be honest—"

I stop myself. There's no way I plan to admit my distance from God lately to her. Like with everyone else, it's better to act like everything's fine. I take a deep breath, then let it out slowly before continuing. "Okay, deal. I'll start."

She gives me a nod of encouragement. "Go on."

"Can I start by just asking for prayer without telling you what it's specifically for?"

Kristin leans forward and embraces me again.

What's with this girl's infatuation with hugs?

"You got it. No details necessary. I'll be praying," she says. "You can do the same for me."

I WAS WRONG.

Scott's all in for the article about risk-taking teenagers and makes a beeline toward me during journalism to let me know.

I'm slouched over my laptop, researching the top social media influencers—which has nothing to do with an article for the school newspaper and everything to do with wasting time until class is over—when Scott marches up.

Scott doesn't know how to be casual about anything. He can be summed up in one phrase: he's always racing around and talking a hundred miles per hour, has boundless energy, and is the most prolific multitasker I've ever seen in the teenage world. I guess that's why he makes such a great editor.

"Alli, I liked your idea about teen risk-takers. Can you have something ready in the next week or so?" He says all that before he's even five feet from my table. He doesn't start off with, "Hey, Alli. How's it going?" or, "Yo, Alli, are you busy?" Nope. Scott's all business.

I unroll myself from the unflattering slouch and snap my laptop closed. I don't want him getting nosy about what I was "researching."

"Oh, hey, Scott. Um, yeah, I guess. I mean, it was just an idea. It doesn't even have to be me who writes it. We were just hashing out some ideas at the meeting on Friday."

He doesn't even look at me but studies a group at another

table who's going over a page layout—probably already rearranging their idea in his head—and taps his pencil on the table surface near my elbow.

"No, I think you'd do great with it." Scott peels his gaze back to me. "See if you can include a real-life scenario with the story to really drive home the point, stir up the reader's emotions. You know."

I plaster on a smile even though I'm curious about the "you know" he threw in there at the end. "Well, okay. I'll see what I can do."

With one last tap of his pencil, Scott's off to the layout table.

I stare at his retreating back. I could—no, I *should*—kick myself.

Why couldn't I have suggested the risk-taking consequences of social media influencers? That would've been way more interesting.

Chapter Seventeen

I'VE BEEN STARING at my laptop for ten minutes now, trying to find a starting point for my article on risk-taking teenagers and not having much luck. I've done some online research, but most of the sources are written by psychologists or parenting agencies. I'm looking for something more exciting and relatable to my audience: my peers.

Writer's block is in full force.

The soft knock on my bedroom door is a welcome distraction. I already know it's Avery because she has this timid knock that sounds like she's sorry to bother you but is going to do it anyway.

"Come in, Avery."

She's already dressed in her long, flannel nightgown and fuzzy slippers, and it's still two hours before her bedtime. But knowing Avery, she's probably been in her pajamas since she got home because changing into comfortable clothes is usually the first thing she runs to do after school every day.

"What are you working on?" she asks, kicking off her slippers before crawling across my bed to curl up next to me.

That's one thing I really love about Avery. She's so laid back and easy to be around. Not like most kid sisters—or cousins, in my case—who make it their objective to annoy you and be in your business all the time. I usually don't mind her hanging out in my room, and I've even let her stay the night with me a time or two.

I sigh and set the laptop aside. "Nothing. At least that's what I have so far on an article I'm supposed to write."

I grab my phone off the end table and start browsing social media. Avery adjusts her pillow so she can watch my screen. I look down into her wide, brown eyes and give her a scolding look. "Kind of nosy, aren't you?"

She grins and punches my thigh. She knows I don't mean it.

I scoot down on my pillow so she can see better, and we spend the next twenty minutes looking at photos and stories, commenting about cute outfits, and laughing at dumb memes. We watch a short video of a guy pranking his girlfriend and then scroll on to the next picture.

It's a photo of Tessa and some guy next to a large lake. I make out a full moon hovering over some tall trees behind them and several other teenagers nearby sitting around a large campfire.

I can't remember the last time Tessa even posted anything on social media, and I stare down at the picture like it's about to leap up and grab me by the throat. The fact that Tessa's sitting on the guy's lap is probably the real source of my shock.

Tessa definitely has a daring side to her, but she rarely shows it to people she doesn't know very well. I've never seen this guy she's with and can't help but wonder how *she* knows him.

She isn't all over him or anything—just barely perched on the end of his knee and smiling at the camera. It's just that Tessa isn't like that at all—at least not the Tessa I know. She doesn't just sit on guys' laps, and she especially wouldn't want a picture of it posted on social media. But she and the guy are both staring right at the camera, giddy as can be, so she obviously doesn't care about the photo being shared with the world.

Looking closer, I notice that one of the other teenagers is holding an amber-colored bottle, but everyone in the background is too blurry for me to recognize who they are. I'm sure there's alcohol and who-knows-what-else at this get-together. Even though it shouldn't bug me anymore, I can't help but worry about Tessa.

Why do I care what she does after how she's treated me? I think.

But I do care. And I don't know why. I guess old habits are hard to break.

Avery squints and leans into the photo. "Is that Tessa with that guy?"

Oops. I meant to scroll past it before she recognized Tessa.

"Uh, yeah. I guess she was hanging out with some friends from school."

Avery leans hard against my shoulder now as she peers closer at the picture. "Whoa, that's kind of—"

I jam my elbow into her side. "Don't say it."

She rolls her head back to look up at me. "Why don't you guys hang out anymore? Are you two fighting?"

I'd love to unload everything on Avery right now and have another ally on my side, but she's only nine and too young to understand. Besides, I'm supposed to be the mature older sister and the example.

I don't feel like playing any of those roles right now, but I keep my mouth shut. "I guess we've outgrown each other," I say. "I think we just need some space for a while."

"Are you still friends, though?" Avery points at the picture frozen on my phone screen. "Is that Tessa's boyfriend?"

I don't want to tell her that high school's like being on another planet and that just because a girl sits on a guy's lap doesn't mean they're dating. I don't want her to think that's how I go around behaving, even if that's how she sees Tessa in this photo. Avery doesn't see that kind of stuff in fourth grade —at least I *hope* she doesn't. Who knows what kids are exposed to anymore? Still, it's clear she knows something doesn't feel right about it.

I scroll past the picture. "I have no idea, Avery. Tessa and I don't really talk anymore, so I don't know if she has a boyfriend or not."

I set the phone down on the bed and nudge her with my foot. "Alright, twerp. Get outta here. I've got homework to finish."

But Avery isn't done yet. She sits up and crosses her legs, facing me. "Do you like any guys at school, Alli?"

I don't bother trying to hide my scowl. "No, Avery. I don't. I wouldn't date any of the guys at my school anyway."

"Because they aren't Christian?"

I guess we're going to be here a bit longer. My article will have to wait. It's not like I was making progress on it anyway.

Drawing my knees to my chest and wrapping my arms around them, I think about how to answer her. I've been raised to believe that dating and marriage should only be with someone who shares my faith—that trying to have a relationship outside of that boundary will only end up in heartache and conflict. Now that I'm old enough to choose my own path and work through my faith myself, I still believe that it's true. But that doesn't mean I don't struggle with it. There are a lot of cute guys at my school, and there have even been a few I've flirted with, but that's as far as it's ever gone.

Avery stares at me, obviously waiting for me to answer.

"Yeah, that's part of it," I finally say. "But honestly, I'm not looking for a boyfriend right now anyway."

"What if Anthony asked you out?"

It takes me a second to figure out who she's talking about, but then I realize she's talking about the only guy my age she knows by that name. She wouldn't know anyone from my school.

"Anthony from church?" I ask. "And where did you pick up this talk about guys asking girls out? Is this what girls talk about at recess nowadays instead of playing hopscotch?"

Avery giggles. "Some of the girls talk about boys, but I don't. I just listen. And, yes, silly. I mean Anthony from church. Who else would I be talking about?"

"Seriously, Avery?"

I look around for something to throw at her and end up grabbing a throw pillow.

She laughs and dodges the pillow. "What?! He's cute!"

Her giggle is so contagious that I can't help but join her.

"Of course, he'd be cute to *you*," I say. "You think all guys older than twelve are cute. Especially if he smiles at you and lets you play on his team for volleyball, like *Anthony* does."

On youth nights at the park, we play volleyball a lot, and Anthony always invites Avery to be on his team, even though she misses the ball more than she hits it. That's just how nice of a guy he is. I wouldn't even be surprised if my nonna was still here and developed a crush on him.

Avery scoops up the throw pillow and launches it back at me. "Well, who *do* you like?"

"What makes you think I have to like *anyone*? There are more important things in life than guys, you know."

I'm surprised to see the mischievous twinkle in Avery's eyes dim as she snatches another pillow from the bed and hugs it to her. Her expression turns sad, and I start to worry she has an awful confession to make that I'm not sure I want to be the first to hear.

"Alli, are you going to go away to college next year?"

I'm surprised by the sudden change of topic and wonder what caused it. "Whoa, aren't you full of questions tonight? First the boyfriend, and now you want me out of the house. Do you really want my bedroom that bad?"

I give her a playful shove and see a subtle lift in the corner of her mouth, even though I know she's trying to be serious.

"Nah, my room's closer to the bathroom. I just wanna know."

"Why?"

"Because . . ." She shrugs.

"Because . . . why?"

When her chin tucks down into the pillow and she turns those big, puppy-dog eyes up at me, I know she needs to talk about something. It was probably the real reason she dropped by my room in the first place.

"Well, I don't know," she says. "I just don't want you to, you know, leave."

Her comment hits like a well-placed dart between my ribs. I don't need to read between the lines, because I know exactly what Avery's showing me. She rarely lets her guard down when it comes to some of the fears she struggles with since her mom passed away. But I know from other girl-talk nights that Avery still struggles with losing her mom and is afraid of losing others in her life that she loves.

I hold my arms out to her, and she doesn't hesitate. Dragging the pillow with her, Avery snuggles up against me and rests her head on my chest. It's times like these that I remember being her age and needing my mom's reassuring hugs.

I can't even begin to understand what Avery must feel like losing her mom when she was so young. It was devastating enough for the rest of the family, much less for a six-year-old girl. As I run my fingers down her long, brown hair, I'm so grateful that Avery at least had the comfort of living with family after facing that.

"You can't get rid of me that easily, sis," I say, giving a strand of her hair a gentle tug.

She doesn't answer.

I don't really expect her to. I'm just making small talk, trying to tiptoe around the elephant that somehow snuck into the room.

I sigh as I lay my head back on my pillow. "I don't even know what next week looks like for me, Avery, much less next year. I'm just going to have to trust God to show me what to do when the time comes. But whatever happens, I promise that I'll always be here if you need me. Okay?"

She gives my waist a squeeze and shuffles off the bed. At the door, she turns around and smiles. Avery looks back to her old self, and I'm glad. I don't know what we would've done if both of us had started bawling.

"So . . . do you think Anthony is at least cute, though?"

She's out the door before I can reach for another pillow to throw.

Chapter Eighteen

I'M SITTING on a low concrete wall waiting for the first-period bell when I hear someone come up behind me. Swinging around, I find myself looking up into Chad Barton's face. I'm so shocked that I almost drop the book I was reading.

His grin tells me that he noticed.

"Hey, what's up?" He says it so casually. As if we hang out all the time instead of the reality of only having spoken to each other when I interviewed him for the school newspaper.

I snap the book closed—only briefly disappointed that I didn't save my place—and shrug, even though my heart pounds in my chest.

"Hey, Chad. Uh, nothing much. You?"

He walks over and sits a few feet away on the wall, shoving his backpack down to the ground between his legs and resting his elbows on his knees. He looks as casual as I am nervous.

I glance around to see if any of his friends are close by and wonder if Chad was just looking for a place for them to sit and hang out before school starts. But there are only two girls standing nearby taking selfies and giggling. Probably freshman from the way they're carrying on.

What's he doing here? I wonder.

I look back at Chad, who sits up and stretches, a big smile breaking out across his face. "I had to meet with the coach this morning, so I'm here a little early," he says. He nods at the book I'm clutching against me to hide my trembling hands. "Whatcha reading?"

I pull the book away and look down at it like I've never seen it before. I'm sort of wishing that were true because I suddenly feel like a nerd sitting alone and reading a book instead of hanging out with friends like other non-nerd girls do. It's not even a cool book—like some popular, utopian, young adult fiction everyone raves about and that's so popular they're thinking of making a movie based on it. No, it's not that cool at all.

"Oh, um, it's . . ." Maybe I've lost my nerve and my voice simultaneously, because I turn the book around and just show it to him instead.

He reads the title aloud. "*The Scarlet Letter.* Sounds ominous. Is that required reading for English Lit this year?" His dark blue eyes dance with some kind of secret delight in watching me squirm. He probably has that effect on all the girls.

"No, it's just something I picked up that looked interesting," I fib. The truth is that it's probably, like, the fourth time I've read this book. But there's no way I'm admitting that.

A high pitch clang echoes over the courtyard, signaling the

beginning of the school day, and I jam the book down into my backpack, stand, and swing the backpack over my shoulder so fast that it's Chad's turn to jump in surprise.

Flicking my ponytail back over my shoulder with one hand, I give a lame wave with the other and start backing away.

"Well, I'll see you around," I say, while an internal battle of *Stay. No, go!* rages back and forth in my brain.

A thousand ballerinas pirouette across my stomach when Chad stands and grabs his backpack. "I'll walk you to class."

I don't remember much of what we talk about during the two minutes it takes for him to walk me to first period. But I feel myself floating on a cloud that somehow leads to my chair in Mr. Ankor's class just as he makes his morning announcement about picking up our worksheets on the back table.

Staring down at my paper a few minutes later, I replay the scene with Chad in my head from beginning to end, trying to catch anything stupid I said—and I come up with plenty of things—or imagine if my facial expressions seemed natural and not as panicky as my insides felt.

Bits and pieces of the conversation on our way to class come back to me. Something about him asking if I ever attend the football games and what I like to do with my free time. For the life of me, I can't remember what my answers were. I hope and pray they were at least coherent.

It's Chad's last words that really tie my nerves in knots: "I'll catch you later."

What does that mean? Did he just throw it out there as a casual parting phrase, or did he really mean he would catch up with me later? As in, he plans to actually talk to me again?

My anxious internal dialogue is interrupted by two girls sitting behind me who are talking about a party going on this Friday night. I would normally eavesdrop so I can catch all the juicy details to share with Tessa later, but I won't be talking to Tessa later, so what's the point?

I look down at my blank worksheet and attempt to read the directions for the third time when one of the girls starts rattling off some of the popular kids' names who would be there, and I hear Chad's name come up. The girl doesn't say his last name, but I'm pretty sure she means Chad Barton because he's right up there with the "in" crowd, and he's the only Chad I even know at West Morrison High.

Just as soon as I tune in to eavesdropping mode to find out more, Mr. Ankor gets up from his desk, and the two girls clam up and act interested in their work.

I try to refocus, so I don't end up having this assignment as homework, but halfway through matching European colonization terms with their definitions, my mind starts to wander again. One or two thoughts stand out the most from all the others competing against each other in my brain.

The ones that scare and thrill me at the same time are: *Why did Chad Barton come around this morning? Why in the world would he dare to be seen walking me to class?*

I DON'T KNOW WHY, but I have a sick feeling in my stomach as Brynne walks over to Tessa's table to ask her if she wants to be lab partners.

Tessa's sitting alone, but that's probably just because Shanice is always late to class and hasn't shown up yet. I guess Brynne figures that since she and Tessa were partners before, Tessa might be cool with the idea. But Brynne hasn't figured out yet that Tessa isn't the same person she was a few weeks ago when they teamed up as partners. In fact, I'm not even sure who Tessa is anymore myself.

I feel bad about the whole situation. Brynne was absent yesterday, so Zach and I teamed up, and we're already halfway through our experiment. Otherwise, I would've offered to work with her. Zach wouldn't have cared. There are plenty of other guys in the class he could've partnered with.

From my seat, I see Tessa glare at Brynne like Brynne just ran over her puppy with her bike. It's obvious Tessa's brushed her off by the way she's shaking her head and giving Brynne a dirty look.

From the corner of my eye, I catch Shanice flouncing in just as Brynne shrugs and starts to walk away. In typical obnoxious fashion, Shanice crows from two tables away, "Oh, my gosh. What's with those *shoes*?" as she stares wide-eyed down at Brynne's feet.

Naturally, most of the kids turn to see the commotion, and the back of the room where I'm sitting grows quiet. Even Zach pauses with his pencil in the air.

I can't help it; I lean back in my chair and sneak a peek at Brynne's shoes. She's wearing swirled, pastel-colored platform boots that lace up over her ankles. The shoes add at least two inches to her height.

Personally, I think they're totally cool, and I hear several others sitting nearby agree. And if she wasn't just looking for something to cause drama over, Shanice would probably think so too.

Tessa starts giggling and makes a show of looking under the table to check them out. Brynne stands like a concrete statue, her eyes following Shanice as she seats herself next to Tessa.

"Wow, Brynne," Tessa chimes in. "Did your blind neighbor paint those shoes for you? I get dizzy just looking at them."

Shanice busts out laughing, and I hear someone whisper, "Ah, that's cold, girl."

But by the way Tessa and Shanice carry on, it's obvious neither of them cares. They're like sharks on a feeding frenzy, totally oblivious or just too cold-hearted to notice that Brynne hasn't said a word. Her platform boots are glued to the floor, and I feel the need to go rescue her, despite the fact that I would be putting myself in Shanice's direct line of fire.

And Tessa? Would she back down if I got involved? I'm curious how far Tessa would go with me if I called her out too.

Just as I start to slide off my chair, Mr. Martin hollers for everyone to sit down. Brynne unglues herself and makes her way back to our table. Her face is beet red, and her mouth looks like a tight ball of wax as she yanks her chair back and throws herself down on it, kicking her backpack out of the way under her.

I jerk my head toward Mr. Martin so Brynne has at least one less set of eyes ogling her. Clearly, Zach doesn't take the hint, and I give him a little kick under the table to break him out of his trance. I think he's still a little clueless about what's going on.

"Zach, are you ready to get started on the experiment?" I ask in a low warning voice just in case he decides to start asking questions.

Zach shrugs and reaches for his notebook. "Yeah, I got everything." He looks over at the empty place in front of me. "Where's your notebook?"

"Oh, yeah." Even though I try not to look over at Brynne and want to give her some space, I catch a glimpse of her texting on her phone as I reach down for my notebook.

Zach and I work on our experiment, leaving Brynne to herself. I let Zach take most of the notes because he's more organized than me. Besides, I'm too distracted right now to focus. I glance over at Brynne a few times and see her writing in her notebook. I don't know if she's writing something science-related or just pouring out her rage on paper, but she doesn't have any lab supplies in front of her.

Mr. Martin never comes our way, so he doesn't notice.

I decide not to say anything to Brynne until about five minutes before class ends and we're cleaning up and putting supplies away. When Zach walks away with his hands full of jars and tubes, I turn to her.

"Hey, Brynne. That was messed up of Shanice and Tessa."

Brynne looks up from her notebook and shrugs. "Yeah, now I see why you don't hang around Tessa anymore," she says, turning to glare at Tessa's back across the room.

"Do you want to hang out for lunch again today?" The words are out of my mouth before I realize it.

Brynne accepts with a grateful smile.

Not caring if Tessa and Shanice are looking our way, I make

it a point to walk with Brynne out of class. I secretly hope Tessa dares to say something to me so I can show up at her house—where she'd be away from her posh, snobby friends—and confront her with all this baloney she's been dishing out for weeks now.

I don't care if she doesn't want to talk to me anymore or that our friendship is a thing of the past, but I'm not going to stand around and put up with her using me or anyone else for target practice. Even if she doesn't care what I have to say, at least I'll have said it.

Chapter Nineteen

BRYNNE and I hang out at school all week. She makes me laugh and she's a lot of fun to be around once you get to know her. Tonight's the first time I've invited her over to my house, though.

My mom was surprised when I asked if I could invite a friend from school over, but she shocked me just as much by asking if I wanted my friend to stay for dinner too. The best part of the whole deal is that Brynne has her own car and drives us to my house instead of having to walk like I usually do. *Score!*

Over dinner—thanks to my dad's barrage of curious questions and natural ability to make everyone feel like he's their favorite uncle—I learn that Brynne's dad is in the Air Force and travels a lot. She also tells us her mom teaches drama at the middle school a couple blocks from my house.

Later, when we're sitting in my room, it's Brynne's turn to

learn more about me. She starts by asking what everyone seems to get around to asking sooner or later.

"So, you're a Christian, right? Where do you go to church?" she asks, watching me sit on the floor and plait my long hair into a braid.

"Tucson Apostolic," I say. "My family's been going there since I was a little girl. What about you? Do you go to church?" I flick my braid over my shoulder and lean back against the leg of the desk chair, resigned to the direction the conversation is going. It's only natural that people are curious.

"Nah," Brynne answers. "I'm not a Christian. I mean, not really. My family goes to church a few times a year when my grandma's church has special services for holidays, and her pastor officiated my uncle's funeral last year. But we aren't official members of any church." She gives me a pointed look. "Don't get me wrong. We aren't atheists or anything."

A nervous laugh bubbles out, and she takes a quick sip of her drink before continuing. "I knew you went to church and all because I heard you making plans with Tessa one day in science, and you told her you couldn't go somewhere because you had to go to Bible study that night," she says. "Tessa was like, 'Oh, yeah, I forgot.' I figured by her answer that it must be a regular thing."

I know this is my cue to take the stage and launch into a script about my faith and maybe invite her to church, but I find myself at a loss for words. Sure, I've put my faith out there lots of times, and I've never been uncomfortable about being a Christian, but I don't feel like talking about it tonight.

I'm disappointed in myself for dropping the ball on a

golden opportunity with Brynne, but the urge to just be known for being "Alli, the *cool girl* from science class," instead of "Alli, the *Christian girl* from science class," is stronger than my desire to obey my heart.

I'm tired of explaining why I'm different. It just makes everything awkward and I start to feel like that odd puzzle piece all over again.

Or maybe I'm made up of a bunch of puzzle pieces, all with different labels on them. The struggle overwhelms me. Sometimes, I just want to take the whole thing, throw it off a bridge, and watch the pieces float away with the current.

"So . . . church is a pretty big deal with your family then, huh?" Brynne asks, dragging me from the fog of my thoughts.

"Yeah, going to church is a big part of my life," I mumble lamely. "So . . . do you think Zach is cute?" I quickly change the subject, ready to move on.

Brynne's mouth drops open, and we both start giggling. "Whoa. That was random," she says. "Nerdy Zach? You're joking, right? Eww . . ."

"Well, I think he's kinda cute—in a geeky kind of way." I shrug, another giggle escaping. "I think he likes you, though."

Brynne's eyes widen and one hand goes to her chest. "Well, he's definitely not my type, so why don't *you* go for him, Alli?"

"Nope, not happening." I shrug. "He's not my type either."

"I didn't think so," she says. "Who *would* you go for? Trevor? Isn't he more your type?" She wiggles her eyebrows.

"If you're talking about Trevor from economics, he already

has a girlfriend. Nice try." I smirk. "And exactly what do you think my *type* is?"

Brynne slides off the bed to join me on the floor and hugs her knees to her chest, a reflective look on her face. "Hmm, I brought up Trevor because his dad's a pastor. I guess I could see someone like him with you because you both go to church and aren't wild and don't party like everyone else."

She leans back and tucks a fist against her hip, head cocked to one side. "Unless you're a secret wild child no one knows about."

I laugh and decide I'd better not mention that I *have* snuck out to spy on other people's parties like a creepy stalker. I'm betting Tessa has kept that bit of info to herself too since it would make her look like a freak if her new friends knew she was spying on their parties.

"Yeah, I'm a total wild child, Brynne," I say, my voice low and menacing. "You probably shouldn't even hang out with me, because I might lead you down a dark path."

It's fun to laugh with someone again. I didn't realize how much I've missed hanging out with a friend and sharing girl talk. I've been stuck in the house every day after school for weeks, except for going to church or other places with my family. Even my mom's been casting worried looks my way, like she's afraid I'm turning into a hermit with social anxiety or something.

Brynne and I talk for a few more minutes before she needs to go home. I'm disappointed the night's already over. When she finally leaves, I watch from the window as she gets into her car and drives away.

The house feels empty, even though it's not. Mom and Dad went to bed hours ago and Avery's holed up in her room, probably pretending to be asleep but really reading a book under the covers with her book light, which she does almost every night. But the silence in the room feels like a heavy blanket on my shoulders.

Maybe I do need a friend, after all.

I HEAR the *chirp* from my phone on the nightstand next to my bed just as I'm starting to fall asleep. Knowing it's past 11:00 p.m. because I'd just looked at my phone at 10:56, I roll over and snatch it up, tugging the charger out since it doesn't reach across my bed.

Who in the world is texting me at this time of the night?

The bright glow of the screen blinds me for a second before I can focus. Then, I see Tessa's name on the notification before I read, **Can I call right now?**

I slide over on the notification to reply, **Sure.**

I scoot my body up from under my comforter and lean against the headboard while I wait to accept her call.

My mind races through scenarios: *Are her friends all busy tonight and she's calling me because she's bored?* I glance toward my closet. *Do I still have one of her shirts or a jacket she needs me to bring her tomorrow?*

I can't think of one logical reason Tessa would be calling me. I spend the next minute flipping through potential scenarios in my imagination before my phone comes alive with the song, "You've Got a Friend in Me"—my ringtone for Tessa.

I need to change that ringtone later.

I put the phone to my ear. "What's up?" I try to sound casual, like we talked just yesterday instead of weeks ago. My heart pounds in my chest.

"Hey," Tessa says, her voice low and somber.

I don't say anything else, giving her the floor. She's the one who made the call.

"Sorry to wake you." Tessa's the only one who would know that I'm probably the only senior in high school who goes to bed before eleven o'clock at night.

"It's cool." Again, I don't throw her a lifeline, but curiosity pokes at me like a safety pin that's come undone under my clothes.

The silence drags on so long that I pull my phone away to make sure we're still connected.

Impatience creeps in while I wait for Tessa to say more. I hear her soft breathing on the other end of the line and the dread that this could be a stupid prank call she's pulling off and that her new friends are listening in starts to coil around my chest.

I'm about to ask if she called for a reason other than to just breathe in my ear when I think I hear a faint sniffle. I give in. "Tessa? Are you okay?"

"No, not really." Her voice is so soft that I'm having a hard time understanding her. "There's a lot going on in my life right now. I just . . . it's so much pressure." Her voice catches in a sob. "I really don't even know why I'm calling you, Alli. I know you don't want to talk to me right now."

I'm struck dumb for a moment. Even if I *did* want to talk to her, it would take me a minute to make the words come. I'd rehearsed telling Tessa off a thousand times, and I had a tidy speech all prepared to throw in her face should this moment come but, suddenly, I can't remember a word of it.

"Well, I'm calling anyway," Tessa continues. "We've been best friends for years, Alli. You know me better than anyone else. I just thought . . ."

Her voice sounds funny, and how she's carrying on is a bit dramatic for Tessa even on her worst days. I'm not sure whether to pity her or be irritated.

"Tessa, have you been drinking?"

She doesn't answer right away. When she does, I sense the tension in her voice. "Wow, Alli, that's low. What's that got to do with anything I'm saying? I called you because I needed a friend. Especially with my dad moving out and all."

She breaks down with her last words, and my irritation vanishes. Since she'd walked out of my life, I hadn't thought much about Tessa's family. The family trouble Tessa had shared with me before had been pushed to the back burner.

"Wow. No way. I'm so sorry, Tessa. I know you said things weren't too great and that your parents might divorce, but I didn't know it was that bad already. Your dad moved out? That must be super hard on you guys."

Tessa's parents have always been like a second family to me, and I can't even begin to imagine them being separated. Tessa and I had never really had the chance to finish the conversation about what was going on at home. I feel awful for her, and I'm sure she's only pouring it all out to me now because she's probably been drinking—most likely at one of those stupid parties with her new, less-than-stellar friends. Who knows what kinds of things she's letting herself get dragged into.

Tessa doesn't answer, but I can hear her muffled sniffing behind a tissue or something she's holding to her face.

"You still there?" I ask.

"Yeah, I'm here," she mumbles. "It's been awful. Mom cries all the time now, and Aaron won't talk to anyone. He just locks himself in his room every day after school."

My heart goes out to her even though I'm still raw from her recent distance and rejection. I can't help but ask because it's bothering me. I'm only human. "Gosh, Tessa. I don't know what to say. I mean, I'm honored that you still trust me and that you're sharing this with me, but, well, have you told any of this to Shanice or Kim?"

I bite my lip as soon as the words are out. I know it's a cheap shot and, honestly, I'm kind of surprised I dared to ask. Maybe I'm harboring more bitterness over this situation than I realize.

"No. I'm not telling them my family's problems, Alli. They wouldn't get it." She sighs and yawns softly, but her voice remains sad. "We don't talk about stuff like that. Like I said . . ." She hesitates. "It's a lot of pressure. I can't explain it."

I want to remind her that *she's* the one who walked away and abandoned me like a used dishrag. I wrestle with genuine sympathy over what her family's struggling with, but it's overpowered by self-preservation. I also stew over the possibility that she *has* been drinking and that the person on the other end of the phone is an alcohol-diluted version of Tessa. The *real* Tessa will probably regret calling me tomorrow.

Just before I come up with a tactful way to say, "I told you so," I hear a timid whisper on the other end of the line. Her voice is still barely above a whisper, so I ask her to repeat it.

"Would you pray for me, Alli?"

Chapter Twenty

COULD this day get any worse?

First off, there's no body soap in the shower. That would be Avery's fault since she's the only other person who shares the hall bathroom with me. I have to use shampoo instead, which leaves me feeling gross. Then, I snag my sweater on a cabinet handle, and I'm forced to run back to my room and change.

If all that wasn't irritating enough, in my hurry to not be late for school, I forget my lunch on the kitchen counter and only have enough cash to buy a bag of chips and a soda from the snack bar.

But on a good note, I'm starting to enjoy eating lunch alone by the library. I discovered an old, wooden bench under a tree near the side entrance that I'm pretty sure everyone has forgotten even exists. And, after brushing off a layer of fossilized bird droppings, I made it my own thirty-minute escape from humanity during lunch break.

That's where I'll be heading today after I grab my pathetic excuse for a lunch. I know I could ask Brynne to eat with me, but I'm feeling melancholic and don't want to be around anyone. I'm also tired because I couldn't go back to sleep for a long time after the phone call with Tessa last night.

After paying for my chips and soda, I make my way to the cart where the utensils and napkins are rolled out at lunch. Just as I reach to pull a napkin from the dispenser, a hand reaches around me and smacks down on top of the metal cart, a thundering *praaang* filling the air.

I almost jump out of my skin. Then, a voice growls next to my ear, "That will be five dollars first, missy."

I spin around and get ready to lay into the idiot who dares invade my space, but come face-to-face with none other than Mr. Heartthrob, Chad Barton, himself, and the steam of my anger simmers to tepid.

Chad grins down at me while I stand there processing just how close to me he really is. In fact, he's so close that I'm instantly intoxicated by whatever fantastic body spray he's wearing.

"Oh, um, it's you . . . Hey, Chad," I say.

"Excuse me," a voice behind us mutters. A girl pushes against me, effectively sandwiching me in between her and Mr. Heartthrob, making the whole situation even more uncomfortable, and grabs two ketchup packs before moving away.

In one swoop, Chad plucks several napkins from the dispenser and moves aside. It's then that I realize we're blocking several people's access to the cart.

"Come with me." Chad motions toward the double doors

leading out of the cafeteria. I have no choice but to follow since, well, he *does* have my napkins, and it's not like he gives me the opportunity to protest.

We make our way past several tables, and I hear people calling out Chad's name several times in greeting. He takes it all in stride, waving back at them like a local celebrity while I follow along dumbly like the fangirl that I am.

Chad glances back and notices that I'm falling behind his long stride and slows down to give me time to catch up. As if the cloud I'm floating on could get any loftier, I find that I'm no longer just following Chad Barton, but am now walking *with* him—as in *next* to him—as if I belong here. If I were to look over at the glass windows we pass, I'm positive my reflection would show a girl with a look on her face akin to a drunk cartoon character.

I shake my head and try to look more natural.

Where in the world are we going? is the first question running through my mind. And right on its tail is, *Why is Chad Barton asking me to follow him?*

I'm puzzled beyond words and delightfully honored to be following one of the most popular guys in school *at his request*, but I'm also starting to feel baffled about the whole deal. I'm sure people seeing us walking together right now are just as baffled as I am.

After stepping around a group of girls sprawled out on the sidewalk drawing on poster board, and then dodging an incoming basketball someone tossed to Chad that he sent back with a volleyball serve, the crowd starts to thin out. We leave the open courtyard and head toward the back side of the science building and the sidewalk that's parallel to the library.

Chad adjusts his pace to mine and looks over at me. "Are you always this quiet?"

Like I could've said anything he would've heard as we walked the red carpet of fame across the middle of the campus.

"Not always," I say. "Mostly when I don't know someone very well." I lift my eyebrows and incline my head to indicate that I mean him, although I'd think that would be glaringly obvious.

I look ahead and notice he's directing us right toward the bench where I've been eating lunch every day. *My* bench. "Where are we going?" I ask.

He nods to the bench. "Isn't that where you usually sit?"

Before I can ask how he knows where I sit to eat lunch every day—which is kind of creepy—he nudges me with an elbow and chuckles. "Relax. I haven't been stalking you or anything. I just see you walking over this way every day and figured out where you were going. I thought I could sit with you today and we could get to know each other better."

Get to know each other better?

I glance around, thinking that there might be hidden cameras in the bushes or that some guy's going to leap from behind a tree, hand Chad five bucks, and say, "Dude, you won the bet."

But when I look back at Chad, he's already swinging his backpack off his shoulder and tossing it on the bench. He plops down at one end and throws a leg up on the bench, leaving the other side for me.

I slide my backpack to the ground and perch on the edge of the bench, staring down at the white-and-neon-striped tennis shoe resting near my hip.

I just spent the past five minutes with my heart in my throat and my limbs being numb from all the nervous energy pulsing through them. Now, I'm sitting on the edge of a bench —*my* bench, in *my* secret cove on campus—wondering whose dream I accidentally waltzed into.

I'm also hungry. But I'd rather die than crunch on noisy chips and drop crumbs from my mouth while the Romeo of West Morrison High School sits next to me.

I stare at the tennis shoe for a moment, then look up at Chad. He seems so relaxed, draped across the seat and sitting here next to me like it's no big deal. But it's a *major* big deal to me.

"Why are you really here, Chad?"

I blame my boldness on being hungry. My defenses must be down, and honestly, I just can't stand not knowing any longer why Chad's showing a sudden interest in me. *Is there a rumor going around that I came into a large inheritance or something?*

Chad's leg slides off the bench as he pushes himself up to lean toward me, acting suddenly shy as his gaze drops to his feet. After a moment, he peeks up at me through that endearing dark curl he always has hanging in his face. The endless vortex of his deep, blue eyes mesmerizes me as the rest of the world fades into the background.

"Actually," he draws the word out, like what he's about to say next will be earth-shattering, "I've been wanting to talk to you for quite a while. You know . . . to get to know you better."

I can't help it. I start laughing.

Then, I notice the hurt expression on his face and realize he's not kidding. I forget trying to maintain my prim posture and coy smile and sink lower in my seat. My shoulders hunch as my mouth drops open in what I'm sure is a totally unflattering look.

"Sorry, Chad. But, come on, are you *serious?*"

He nods and looks back down at the ground, his grin making the dimple on his cheek stand out. "Yeah, there's just something different about you that's kind of mysterious and, I don't know . . . attractive."

If someone had told me two weeks ago that Chad Barton, star of the football team with his irresistible smile that drive all the girls mad, one of the most popular guys in our high school, would be sitting alone with me on a remote bench confessing his *attraction* to me and telling me that he wants to get to know me better, I would've accused them of sniffing too much glue.

But here I am—here *we* are—acting out that exact scenario. I don't know whether to freak out and send Chad running down the sidewalk or throw my head on his shoulder and promise him my heart forever.

I'm not sure *what* to do at this point, so I just sit there like a dumb moose until Chad breaks the awful silence by reaching down for the bag of chips sitting next to my backpack, tugging the bag open, and holding it out to me.

"Did I scare you off?" He chuckles, and the tension eases in my chest.

I grab a chip from the bag and nibble on its edge. "Honestly?"

His eyebrows lift in anticipation. "Yeah, you could start with that."

"I don't know what to say, Chad. I'm flattered . . ."

Chad reaches in the bag and grabs a chip, handing it to me like a crown on a golden platter. "So, does that mean you'll go out with me Saturday night?"

Chapter Twenty-One

O F   C O U R S E, I don't go out with Chad Saturday night.

That would make me look too desperate and easy. A girl has to play hard to get, no matter how flattered and completely blown away she is that a guy—one who's way out of her league, at that—says he wants to get to know her better and asks her on a date, all on the same day.

I know I took a chance of offending Chad by not jumping at his offer, but I'm still trying to figure out what his deal is. What if he was just messing with me, and I had blurted out a "Yes!" only to have him say he was just kidding? I hadn't had time to pinch myself after he walked me to class and then ate lunch with me, much less try to consider where Chad's going with all this attention.

He wants to get to know me better? He wants to take me out?

I'm not so naive that I don't ask myself a hundred times an hour, *Why? Why? Why?*

I stop to look in every mirror, trying to see myself through

Chad's eyes and figure out what it is about me that he's suddenly attracted to. Did I make that much of an impression on him during the interview? Was it something I said? The way I smiled?

Chad doesn't give up. He continues dropping in on me between class periods and showing up at the bench during lunch. It gets to where I start taking longer to get my stuff together at the end of class so he can catch up with me. I even start looking for him as I stand in the snack bar line every morning.

We find that we have a lot in common; we both love French fries dipped in Thousand Island dressing and are both afraid of heights. I learn that he gets the hiccups if he drinks soda too fast, and he discovers that I snort when I laugh.

It's a big deal when I finally give him my number so he can text me. Lame, I know. Most girls would've given it out in the first five minutes. But for me, it feels like the next step toward something important between us.

That and the fact that I finally agree to sneak out with him this Friday night. I'll have to fabricate a huge lie to make it happen and risk my parents catching me. Tessa's the only other person in the world who's ever talked me into doing something this brave—or stupid, depending on how you look at it —before.

Avery laughs hysterically on the floor while I curl myself into a twisted pillar with my limbs wrapped around each other in a way I hope accurately represents the phrase on my card. Then, I slowly unfurl my arms and open them skyward with a swaying motion.

Apparently, what I'm doing is nothing even *close* to accurate because Avery's having a laughing fit on the floor, and Brynne looks like she's about to join her. At least Brynne tries to be polite and stifles her laugh behind a pillow, but her red face gives her away.

"Seriously, guys!" I throw my hands in the air and collapse onto the loveseat across from Brynne.

"Okay! Okay! Um . . . a waving flag?" Brynne peeks over the top of the pillow, then throws it at Avery, who catches it and shoves her face into it to muffle her laughter.

I throw Brynne the most disgusted look I can manage.

She leans forward, grabs the white card I've left on the table, and reads it. "Oh! A butterfly coming out of a cocoon!" She smacks a hand against her forehead.

"Sorry, Alli, but how was whatever you were doing supposed to look like this?" She throws the card back onto the table and busts out laughing.

"I'm done with you guys," I say, then burst out laughing too.

Avery, Brynne, and I have been hanging out all night while my parents go out to dinner and grocery shopping. They offered to take us, but none of us were interested. Since it's a school night, Brynne could only stay for a few hours, and I didn't want to spend it running around with my parents.

Instead, we stayed home and made our own homemade pizzas on English muffins with spaghetti sauce, shredded cheese, and ham slices. Avery and I make them all the time, and they're one of our favorite snacks.

It was Avery's idea to play charades. I wanted to prank call people from church. Juvenile, I know, but do we ever really outgrow pranking people? Avery was all for it, but Brynne didn't think it would be that much fun since she doesn't know anyone from our church and wouldn't have a face to go with the voice. I get it. So, charades it was.

I was first, and Avery and Brynne haven't guessed any of the last three I've attempted, including this last butterfly in a cocoon one. Either I'm awful at charades, or they find it more entertaining to watch me make a fool of myself. I vote for the latter.

"So, what's going on with you and Chad?" Brynne's question knocks me off guard, and I look frantically between her and Avery, who's arranging the pillow back on the couch. I give Brynne a panicked head shake, but she misses it—or ignores it.

Avery spins around. "Chad? Who's Chad?"

Brynne looks at me, but there's no way to shake my head again with Avery staring at me now.

"He's a friend from school," I answer, locking eyes on Brynne, hoping she'll take the hint to drop it.

She doesn't. "Oh, yeah, right . . . A *friend* from school." She smirks.

Avery looks between us. I guess it's up to me to play this off. I don't take my eyes off Brynne when I answer. "Yes, a *friend* from school. We hang out sometimes."

Brynne starts to protest, a mischievous look on her face, but I scrunch my eyebrows at her, and she finally takes the hint.

She scoops the game cards up from the table and walks toward the kitchen. "Are there any snacks?" she asks, giving me my out.

But Avery isn't going to let me off that easy. "Does this Chad guy like you?" She plants herself in front of me, wraps her arms around her waist, and waits for my answer.

I can hear Brynne rummaging around in the pantry. I love how she's the one who started this inquisition but is now hiding in the pantry.

"No, Avery. I mean . . ." I don't want to outright *lie* to her. "We just talk."

She stares at me as if she's waiting for me to finish a story that she knows I'm not telling. She's right. And I have no intention of telling her the rest of the story. Not now, not ever.

"We're *just* friends, Avery. Let it go."

I don't wait for her to come up with any more questions or try to wear me down with her scolding looks. I tug on a strand of hair lying on her shoulder and push past her to the kitchen to see what Brynne has come up with.

"I'm with Brynne," I say. "Let's dig out some snacks."

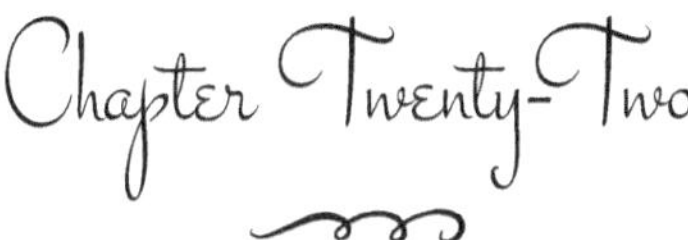

Chapter Twenty-Two

It's the first time I've purposely ditched going to church. It's also the first time I've lied to my parents so I could sneak out with a guy.

There have been a lot of not-so-good-firsts in my life recently.

I tell my mom that I'm not feeling well, which is true because my stomach's such a tight ball of nerves that I think I'm gonna throw up. I can't help it. Saying I'm sick is the only way I can get out of going to church and be able to sneak out with Chad without my parents knowing.

Once a month, we have a special youth service that includes the families. Afterward, everyone plays volleyball or board games and just hangs out. Tonight is volleyball night.

My family looks forward to family night every month and, normally, I do too. So, I need to really play up that I'm feeling terrible to make it believable. I may have been a bit *too* convincing, though, because my mom wavers between digging out crackers and warming a can of soup or staying home with me.

"Mom, I'm not a kid. I'll just be sleeping anyway. Just go," I tell her.

It takes Avery and Dad pitching in to convince her that I don't need someone to stay home and take care of me.

I wait until I hear the truck pull out of the driveway before hopping out of bed, snatching the cute outfit I picked out earlier from the closet, and dashing into the bathroom to change and twist my long hair into a low knot in the back. After curling the loose tendrils around my face and spritzing myself with a floral body spray, I'm ready.

I glance nervously out the window, watching for the lights from Chad's truck. He's picking me up at seven o'clock. I already warned him that I need to be home around nine.

I figured youth service would run at least an hour, and then there would be food and fellowship afterward in the recreation room, and then they'd start picking teams for a volleyball game. My family's usually the last to leave because my mom and dad can talk for hours, and they love to hang out with the other parents over donuts and coffee.

I feel confident I can be back and look like I've been in bed the whole time before they make it home.

I know to probably expect at least one check-in call from my mom, and I'll deal with that when it comes—maybe slip off somewhere quiet and answer with a groggy voice, like I'd been sleeping.

Oh, man, I hope she doesn't suggest that they skip fellowship afterward to come home for me, I realize. I make a mental note to convince her I'm feeling better when she calls.

By the time I slip out the back door at 6:54 p.m., Chad's truck is already parked on the side of the house. He sees me coming and flashes his lights.

"Hey! Right on time!" Chad winks and graces me with his adorable dimples when I jump up into the passenger seat.

My smile is genuine as I latch my seat belt, excited to be on a real date with Chad. My first real date with *any* guy. But we haven't even pulled away from the curb before I start second-guessing myself, wondering if "cool" people think seat belts are only for nerds and hoping I'm not being too obvious that I'm unsure of myself right now.

In the end, I leave the seat belt on and jam my purse down to the floor. My heart thumps hard in my chest until we're around the corner and away from the house.

Chad glances my way and smiles. My anxiety fades when he reaches for my hand.

"Where are we going?" I ask.

I'm hoping I dressed cute enough for tonight. I mean, I don't even know if Chad considers this a real date or if we're just "hanging out." Maybe those both mean the same thing and I'm just clueless. I'm also hoping that Chad doesn't notice how sweaty my hand is becoming.

Not even two minutes into the drive, the fact that I've never gone out with a guy is blatantly obvious. Sitting next to Luis at the youth Christmas banquet last December doesn't count; he didn't even buy my banquet ticket.

Chad guns the accelerator when the light turns green,

pinning me against the back of my seat, and chuckles at the look of panic on my face. "I was thinking of grabbing fast food and heading up to Campbell to enjoy the view while we eat," he says. "But seeing that you have to be home by nine o'clock like a good girl, we don't have time to make it there and back. Wanna hit up Golf N' Stuff for a game of miniature golf instead? We could just grab a bite to eat there."

The "good girl" comment stings. I guess sneaking out behind my parents' backs isn't considered *bad* enough.

"Sure, golfing sounds cool," I say, ignoring the Campbell comment. I'm glad we don't have time to go up the mountain anyway. A game of miniature golf sounds much safer than being alone with Chad, parked at a lookout point above Tucson. I know what other teenagers go up there to do, and a lot of them aren't there just to watch the sunset.

Golf N' Stuff isn't too far of a drive, but my nerves kick back into overdrive. I worry about beating my family home in enough time to undo my hair and look like I've slept the whole time they were gone. I don't dare to even think about what kind of trouble I'd be in if they came home and I'm not there.

There's no way I'm gonna tell Chad all that, though.

I glance down at my purse on the floor and lean over just enough to lift my cell phone halfway from the front pocket to see if there are any notifications. I keep imagining I hear my phone ringing and just pull it out and rest it on my lap, so I'll see it light up if there's a call.

My hand is starting to feel sticky under Chad's and I'm almost relieved when he slips his hand from mine to flick the radio on, then pulls his phone out to search his playlist. An upbeat hip-hop song—one I don't recognize because I don't really listen to that genre of music—pumps through the truck speakers. My heart pulsates with the beat of it.

Everything feels surreal and foreign sitting in a lifted truck with a gorgeous, popular jock from school, sneaking out of the house to be with him, and music blaring from the truck speakers, all while racing down the road at a speed I know is ticket worthy.

I should be soaring on an emotional high of joy from the new adventure. Instead, I feel like the bearded woman at the freak show. It's like a movie, where I know I don't belong in this scene, and that, any moment now, the real actress will show up and send me packing.

But I have to go with it.

I'm here already, and I'd rather die than ask Chad to turn around and take me home where I can pretend none of this happened, slip back into my nightgown, and get back to bed where my family believes I am.

By all the cars jam-packed in the Golf N' Stuff parking lot, I can tell there's no way we're going to be out of here in less than two hours. We'd be crawling behind everyone else in the game.

Chad must be thinking the same thing because he pulls over to the curb, puts the truck in park, and lowers the music. Looking at me, he states the obvious: "It's packed. Maybe we should do something else."

My eyes sweep the parking lot one more time before resting on his eyes, my heart sinking because we're running out of options.

"Yeah, it would take forever to get through here."

I also don't want to confess that, with all these people here, there's a possibility I'll see someone I know who might mention to my parents that they saw me, and . . . well, I don't even want to go there.

"What else can we do?" I ask.

Chad studies a streetlight up ahead, a thoughtful expression on his face while one hand taps out an imaginary tune on the steering wheel.

Suddenly, his head jerks my way and a huge grin covers his face. "I know what we can do! Let's drop by Danny's place." He glances down at his watch. "Things are probably just getting started over there."

I have no idea what he's talking about. "Who's Danny?"

After putting the truck in gear, Chad reaches over and pinches me on the cheek, his eyes dancing with delight. "One of the guys from school. He's got a get-together going on at his place tonight. We can drop by and hang out for a while."

Chad's already pulling out of the parking lot and turning the opposite way from where we came in, assuming I'm game to go along with his idea. "He's chill," he says. Chad looks over and studies my face. He must see my concerned expression because he quickly adds, "Don't worry, Alli. No one's going to be passing out drugs or anything crazy or illegal. I won't be drinking or anything either since I'm driving. You cool with it?"

"Sure, why not?" I shrug and turn my gaze out the window.

I'm not *cool with it* at all, but I don't have the guts to

protest. I tell myself that we're just going to one of his friend's houses to hang out and that it's not a big deal. Chad already said he wouldn't be drinking, and I'm confident I'm not going to see anyone at this party who'd be talking to my parents any time soon. But that doesn't stop my legs from feeling like jelly and my heart from racing.

I should be thrilled that Chad is introducing me to his friends and that it'll be obvious to everyone there that we're . . . together. Whatever *together* means to Chad. We've been hanging out at lunch every day and talking on the phone every night, but are we a *thing*? An *item*? Do I dare ask, or should I just assume we are?

It's not like we're living in archaic times. Guys don't ask girls to "go steady" or to "be their girl" anymore. I feel like such an idiot, but I'm clueless about how one becomes a guy's official girlfriend these days. I never talk about those kinds of things with the girls in my youth group, and I never pay attention to other girls' conversations about them at school. I don't even read romance novels! That's how lost I am.

All I know is I'm not going to paint myself to look like a prude by saying no to dropping in on a simple party. Instead, I ignore the warning sirens going off in my head and the nudge in my heart that I already know is God trying to break through my stubborn will to remind me that I'm treading on dangerous ground.

I know what I'm getting myself into. I've spent this whole roller coaster ride—ever since Chad first waltzed into my life and started showering me with attention—slapping down my conscience and overriding God's nudge to get me back on track. I've been steering myself off the course so much lately that I've lost all sense of where the track even is anymore.

When Chad immediately cranks the music back up after I answer, drowning out all possibility of talking to each other, I'm kind of irritated. I was hoping for some one-on-one conversation since our alone time just got kicked to the curb and we'll be hanging out with a bunch of people I don't know and probably don't care to. They're Chad's friends, not mine. I'm already dreading sticking out like the odd duck in the pond, and I wonder what I could possibly say to these people. People I have absolutely nothing in common with.

When we drive into an upscale neighborhood where everyone has manicured lawns and sports cars in the driveway that cost more than my first year of college will, my fears are confirmed.

Contrary to my cozy neighborhood, where we have only a few styles of houses to break up the monotony, not one house in this neighborhood is like another. We pass a colonial-style mansion that looks like Benjamin Franklin could step out of it at any moment and a gorgeous, cottage-style house that reminds me of a French restaurant.

Finally, we pull up to an immaculate two-story brick house with a curved driveway that's packed full of cars and trucks of every kind, including one or two clunkers. It makes me feel slightly better that at least someone at this party might be on my lower level of the totem pole.

I cringe when Chad steers the truck onto the grass near the side of the driveway to get around a black jeep. I'm sure whoever lives here—Danny, for instance—won't appreciate their lawn being torn up with tire marks. I reach over and turn the music down. Chad winds around the driveway and ends up parking on the gravel under a large tree. Then, he cuts the engine.

"Ready?" he asks, pulling the keys from the ignition and jamming them into his front pocket.

Before I can answer, he's already out of the truck and coming around to my side. I'm mildly impressed that he's gentleman enough to open my door—another checkmark of approval to add to his growing list—but then, instead of opening my door, he moves past it and reaches down under the front truck bumper to pull back a large branch that was brushing up against the grill.

I wait for another second in case he plans to redeem himself, but he keeps moving past the hood of the truck toward the front of the house. I'm still sitting there when he glances back and squints through the windshield to see if I'm coming.

Okay. Guess I'm letting myself out.

I drop my eyes to the phone on my lap and slide it back into my purse, feeling around for a tube of lip balm before tugging on the door handle. When I step out and slam the door, I pull the cap off the balm and apply it to my lips, trying to make it seem like looking for it was what took me so long to get out of the truck.

Chad waits for me, and we walk together to the front porch. Now that we're outside, I'm more aware of the pulsing vibration of music coming from inside the house and surrounding us. By the time we reach the steps, I can't hear most of what Chad's saying to me, but I catch bits and pieces like, "They're laid back," and, "Stick with me." He won't have to tell me twice. I won't be wandering off by myself.

Chad opens the door for me, and I hesitate before entering, wondering why we would just walk into someone's house without knocking first. Chad said he was friends with the guy who lives here, Danny, but it still feels weird just walking in like this. I step over the threshold and walk right into a cloud of cigarette smoke billowing from some guy's mouth and nose next to me, which launches me into a coughing fit.

Great timing. Next time, Chad can walk in first.

The guy—who looks like a long-haired stoner from Woodstock who warped here in a time machine—starts laughing, along with two other guys who are more the jock type with tight T-shirts and dark jeans.

I'm still trying to find my bearings when one of the jocks sees Chad behind me and holds a bottle in the air. "Chad, my man! What's up?" the guy hollers over the music and offers his free hand for a high-five.

Chad slaps it with a *thwack!* "Brock! How's it going?" He punches the guy's friend standing next to him in the arm and gives the stoner a polite nod.

Stoner-guy nods back.

While the male bonding session goes on, I take the time to look around the room and notice all stations of social life sprawled out on the sofa, sitting cross-legged on the floor, standing in clusters around us—basically filling every fiber of area in the spacious room. Suddenly, I feel claustrophobic.

I sense Chad shift toward me and feel a firm arm wrap around my waist. I jerk in surprise.

Chad looks down at me and smiles, oblivious to or ignoring the shocked expression on my face. Turning toward the two jocks—the stoner disappeared somewhere—he pulls me closer.

Somehow, my feet shuffle forward.

"This is Alli," Chad says.

I plaster on a smile. At least, I *think* I'm smiling.

The one called Brock takes a swig from his bottle, then salutes me with it. "What's up, Alli?" Then, looking at Chad, he asks, "How long have you two been a thing?"

Mental note to self: The proper term for being a couple nowadays is "a thing."

I stare at Brock but feel Chad looking down at me.

"We're just friends . . . for now anyway," Chad answers.

Just friends? For now?

The other, unnamed jock grins and winks at me. "Oh, I see how it is." He laughs.

I shoot him a dirty look. He sees how *what* is?

This whole conversation—coupled with the chest-pounding music and the smokey, stale air—is starting to unravel me. I tug on Chad's sleeve and stand on my toes to say in his ear, "Can we move on?"

"Yeah, sure," he answers. He doles out another round of high-fives before leading me through the crowd in the living room and the even bigger crowd in the dining room, greeting people on our way to the backyard.

I reach into my purse to take another peek at my phone. No call from my mom, thank goodness.

I'm between panic mode and nursing a raging headache from all the noise when I spot Tessa. She's hunched down in a lawn chair near an Olympic-sized pool, surrounded by a bunch of guys and a few girls sitting on the grass and in nearby chairs. Shanice sits next to her, texting on her phone.

One of the guys entertains the group with a story or a joke while his audience gives him their full attention, breaking out in raucous laughter a moment later. But my eyes keep drifting to Tessa, who has an amused look on her face but appears to be a thousand miles away. When she reaches down for a bottle on the ground next to her chair, her movement is sluggish and sloppy, and I realize she's probably drunk. *Or high on something.*

An unexpected sadness washes over me as I watch her tip the bottle and drain its contents. I wonder how this night will end up for her. Part of me doesn't even want to go there.

I'm not really concerned that Tessa will notice me since she probably isn't even fully aware of where *she* is right now.

I'm getting tired of being here already. I don't fit in and have no desire to. I've been asked at least eight times in the past twenty minutes if I want a drink, and was hit on by two guys when Chad went to the bathroom (I waited next to a huge stone statue near the edge of the back porch. Well, actually, I was hiding *behind* it.).

That doesn't even count how many girls have hit on Chad while I've been standing next to him. I don't know if I should be flattered that I get to be seen with him or irritated that the fact I'm here with him obviously means nothing to these girls.

To his credit, Chad's included me in all his conversations and has kept his word to not drink anything more than the Coke he's been nursing since we arrived. Unless he poured the Coke in the sink and filled it up with something else when he went to the bathroom.

Let's hope not.

I'm over it—all funned out. I'm so ready to go home and, looking at my watch, we better start that way soon. When Chad's finished listening to some guy's story that I'm pretty sure he's started over three times now, I'll ask him if he's ready to leave.

Then, I hear a voice behind me coo, "Whoa, Chad, I thought you said you weren't coming tonight?"

I can tell by the high pitch, grating sound that it's Kim, Mrs. Queen Cheerleader herself and one of the last people I want to run into right now. I glance back to where Tessa and Shanice are sitting and realize I should've expected that Kim wouldn't be too far behind.

I turn about the same time Chad does. Kim stands there, holding a glass with something clear in it and wearing a skimpy crop top that could pass for a bathing suit piece and cut-off designer shorts that ride low on her hips. A belly button ring catches the light dancing off a nearby tiki torch. Her eyes brush lazily over Chad before drifting to me.

I wait for the look of shock and disdain that I don't plan to back down from, but instead, Kim grins at me.

What's she grinning about?

I assume it means she doesn't realize I came here with Chad and thinks I just happen to be standing here. But, if it dawns on her that Chad and I really are here together, she hides it well.

"Alli, what a surprise," she says. "What's a nice girl like you doing in a place like this?"

She giggles into her glass as she puts it to her lips. Swallowing several sips, she turns back to Chad, a scolding expression on her face. "Are you trying to pollute her, Chad? You naughty boy." She clucks her tongue like a scolding favorite aunt. "Her parents would be heartbroken to know their chaste little girl is at a place like this."

Her eyes drift back to me. "Your parents *do* know you're here, right?" She presses her fingers to her lips with mocking concern.

Chad doesn't play into it. "Chill, Kim. We just dropped by to hang out for a while. We aren't staying long." He wraps a protective arm around my shoulders. "I'm pretty sure she won't be scarred for life after just one night. We aren't even drinking."

Now that Kim brought up the reminder that my parents have no idea that I'm at a party instead of sick in bed, I glance down at my watch and see that it's now close to nine o'clock. I start to panic when I realize that we need to make record time to get me home before my parents.

Checking my phone again, I'm relieved to see that there has been no calls from my mom. I'm not sure if that's a good or a bad sign. I nudge Chad, speaking in a low voice so Kim doesn't hear.

"I'm going to run to the bathroom real quick, but then we need to go. It's almost nine."

He nods and looks up at Kim. "Is Shanice here?"

I let the two of them chat while I rush off to take care of business. I'd better make it quick.

I MAKE my way to where I think I remember seeing the bathroom. *Was it on the other side of the kitchen?*

After finally finding the bathroom, I notice light coming from under the door. I'm hoping whoever's in there isn't puking or anything, because I'm anxious to get out of here, but I can't hold it until I get home. I pace the dark hallway, listening intently for the clicking of the door lock.

I'm ready to forget it and take my chances that I'll make it home when the door swings open, and I'm face-to-face with Tessa.

At first, she doesn't recognize me. It's not like she would've expected me to be here in a million years. Tessa's face is flushed, and her eyes are a little glassy, but she doesn't look as wasted as I thought she was when I saw her sitting by the pool.

It's obvious when recognition comes to her. "Alli?" The light from the bathroom illuminates the hallway and the shock on Tessa's face.

We just stand there staring at each other, neither of us knowing what to say next. I guess Kim isn't the only one surprised to see me here tonight. I can imagine my presence at this party will make for some interesting gossip at school on

Monday. Maybe I'll make the school newspaper: *Alli Mancini Spotted at a Party.*

"Hey, Tessa." It's the best I can come up with.

A girl in a floral mini skirt and flip-flops comes down the hall, and Tessa scoots close to me to let her into the bathroom. When the door closes, Tessa and I are left standing in the dark, the only light coming from the kitchen at the end of the hallway.

"What are you doing here?" she hisses. I can just make out her wide eyes in the shadows, but I don't mistake the stale smell of alcohol on her breath.

"I'm here with Chad. Maybe I should be asking you the same thing. And by the way, you stink, Tessa. I hope you didn't drive yourself here."

She skips over my jab, intent on making her own point. "What are you doing? You're seriously here with *Chad*? You know guys like him only want to use girls to get what they want before they dump them. He's not one of your church boys, Alli."

I guess it's true what they say about alcohol: it tears down your inhibitions and gives you the courage to say whatever you feel. Well, I don't need alcohol to say what I'm thinking.

"Wow, this conversation sounds familiar, Tessa. Since when do you care anyway? What's it to you if I want to spend time with Chad?" I cross my arms in defiance. "Are you implying that there's no way Chad could actually like a girl like me and that I'm only worth *using*?"

I glare at her, challenging her to deny it. "Or maybe you want Chad for yourself and hope to scare me off."

"Be real, Alli. I'm not interested in Chad, but if I was, I'd be more on his level than *you* are." Her words are a low blow, and even Tessa looks shocked by her words. "I didn't mean that the way it sounded," she mumbles.

"Oh? What *do* you mean, Tessa? So, you're so much better than me now? A few months of rubbing shoulders with the big dogs and now you're looking down your nose at everyone? And just so you know, not that it's any of your business, Chad isn't getting any 'use' out of me." I emphasize my words with air quotes while I snarl into her face.

The girl finally walks out from the bathroom and glances our way. Tessa's back is to her, so the girl only sees my face. She must've seen enough to know she'd better keep walking and stay out of it. She turns away and hurries down the hall.

The bathroom door sits open with the light left on, so Tessa and I get a better view of each other. I'm glad because I hope she can see every bit of how serious I am about not backing down.

I can't quite read the expression on Tessa's face, but her temper seems to have cooled off, because now she's staring at me like a puppy she's found in an alley that she doesn't know what to do with.

"What's going on with you, Alli?" she asks. "Aren't you—I mean . . . do your parents even know about Chad or that you're here tonight?"

Throwing my hands in the air, I huff. "I'm so sick of everyone asking me that tonight! It's nobody's business what I'm doing here or who I'm with. Knock it off with the patronizing. It's annoying, Tessa. Besides—"

"Are you listening to yourself right now, Alli?" she interrupts. "I thought Christians didn't hang around this kind of scene."

I'm stunned. I'm positive I would've been less shocked if she'd told me I'd sprouted horns on my head.

"Why would you say that?" The question comes out in a whisper as my fiery temper is doused under the cold water of her words until I'm left feeling like a smoldering pile of ashes. Tessa knocks me down in the first round with her well-placed words. Words that feel bigger than the sky as I stare at her, dumbfounded.

And, if I doubted her state of mind earlier, her next words are as clear as any sober person's.

"Because I know what you stand for, Alli. Or at least what you *did* stand for, and you know this is all wrong. Wrong for you anyway."

Her words deal the final blow as she turns and walks away. I've tapped out and Tessa knows she's won this round.

It's only when my need to relieve my bladder overpowers me that I move my feet and step into the bathroom. I notice the time on my watch as I turn the lock on the door.

It's 9:12.

I'm dead.

Chapter Twenty-Three

BY SOME MIRACLE—BAD choice of words since I *know* God didn't condone me ditching church, sneaking out of the house, and going to a party with Chad—I made it home and back into my nightgown the other night before my family arrived home from church.

They ended up giving one of the new guys in the youth group a ride home and pulled in the driveway barely ten minutes shy of me sneaking back into the house. Our neighbor's dog had just stopped barking at me after sneaking past his gate a few minutes before they pulled in.

Since then, I've been trying to act normal—which means not letting my face or behavior give away my guilty conscience—around my family and at church. It's also what I'm trying to do at the youth committee meeting tonight.

It's our second youth committee meeting and working together has been more fun than I thought it would be. We have a lot of great things planned for this next quarter and, I must admit, Kristin was a good choice for the committee. She'll be spearheading some of the projects coming up, and I'm impressed with her leadership skills. I'm equally impressed with how well she tries to hide the fact that she's helplessly smitten with Anthony.

Honestly, who out of our youth girls *isn't* in love with Anthony?

I can't tell if Anthony feels the same about her because he's always his same friendly, easy-going self with everyone. They *would* be a cute couple—both have friendly, low-key personalities, and they both have their names engraved on their Bibles. I'm not even joking. I mean, it reveals a lot about a person's dedication if they carry something with their name engraved on it, right?

Anthony and Kristin working side by side on youth activities is a match made in Heaven. At least Kristin has her romantic interest in the proper perspective.

I, on the other hand, am the poster child for an imposter—sitting on the youth planning committee while *basically* dating a guy who, according to Chad's own admission, hasn't darkened the door of a church since fourth grade when he went to Sunday mass with his grandmother. The church topic only came up because Chad wanted to know why I'm always busy on Sundays.

And what I mean by *basically* dating Chad is that he held my hand the whole way home, making me totally forget that I'd just had it out with Tessa and was stressing out about my family getting home before me. I think he'd planned on kissing me too by the way he turned to look at me before I had to abandon ship and race into the house. We've also been inseparable at school, meeting up between classes and spending lunch together.

But I'm still not sure how this works, so I don't know if doing all that makes us official or not.

Even when Chad and I sat together on the bench at lunch today, he twirled a loose strand of my hair in his fingers as we talked. I couldn't tell you what we talked about, because I was *way* too distracted by him doing that and with the way he was looking at me. Like I was the only girl in the world who mattered.

So, here I sit, trying to focus on this youth committee meeting when Anthony asks me if I'll check with my mom about heading up the spaghetti dinner fundraiser again this year. My mom does a great job every year and it always pulls in quite a chunk of profit.

"I'm sure she wouldn't mind. I'll check with her." I jot down a reminder in my planner.

"That would be great. Thanks, Alli," Anthony says.

When the meeting's over, I scoop my purse onto my shoulder and grab my can of Coke from the table. Kristin lingers over her calendar, concentrating on jotting down an entry and probably hoping to have a moment alone with Anthony when the rest of us clear out of the room.

Anthony's explaining something to one of the other guys about a flyer he needs for an upcoming event, but he looks over at me just as I'm scooting my chair in.

"Can you hang on a sec, Alli?" he asks.

From the corner of my eye, I see Kristin look my way, cap her pen, and start collecting her things. I'm still looking at Kristin when I answer Anthony. "Uh, yeah. Sure."

Pulling her purse from the back of her chair, Kristin gives a little wave to Anthony, then turns to me.

"Have a great day at school tomorrow, Alli." She hesitates a moment, then melts into the crowd lingering outside in the hallway.

~

"How's it going?"

Anthony pulls out a chair on the other side of the table and lowers himself down into it. The guy he'd been chatting with waves and walks out. It's just Anthony and me left in the room even though the door's open and there's a cluster of teenagers hanging just outside in the hall.

It still feels weird that it's just the two of us.

I sit back down. "Great. Everything's going good."

I realize my head keeps nodding nervously even after I stop talking, so I switch to pulling my sleeves down over my wrists, even though they're already pulled down. "You?"

Of course, Anthony looks completely chill, like he's getting ready to interview me for a job and is taking his time evaluating my stress level. I'm sitting directly under the ceiling fan, and it's making the loose baby hairs around my face dance against my skin. I let go of my sleeve to scratch my neck. I'm waiting for Anthony to go on. The suspense is killing me.

"Nothing much." He shrugs. "My Aunt Sandy's still in the hospital. She's not doing too great, so my mom and I are flying out to see her this week."

I catch the sadness in his eyes before he reaches for a pen laying on the table and starts clicking the top with his thumb. I guess I'm not the only one who fidgets with things when I feel uncomfortable.

"I'm sorry. I had no idea, Anthony."

"Yeah, she seemed better after we had prayer for her Friday night, but then she took a bad turn yesterday. My mom's pretty torn up. She hopes Aunt Sandy will make it until we can get there on Tuesday."

I swallow hard. I would've known there was prayer for her if I'd been there Friday night, but I was too busy sneaking around with Chad instead. Guilt merges in on me from several angles.

"I'll pray for her." At least I'll *try* to, but I don't think it'll help much, since I haven't had much of a connection with God lately.

"Thanks." Smile back in place, Anthony clicks the pen once more and tosses it back on the table. "Anyhow, that's not what I asked you to stay back for. Do you still write for your school newspaper?"

I'm surprised Anthony remembers that detail about me. I never really talk about it at church because I write mostly about school-related topics and goings-on, and no one in my youth group cares about that.

"Yeah, I do," I say. "Why?"

"Well, I was thinking it would be cool if our youth had their own newsletter. It would be a once-a-month thing—just something simple where we could share an event calendar, announcements, our monthly Bible reading chart, and whatever. It would be one page, maybe front and back for busier months." Anthony leans forward, really getting into the idea.

"I was also thinking we could include a short devotional or something, which I was hoping you would write for us. After a while, you could see if any of the other youth, or even one of the adults, want to contribute a devotional or a thought. Would you be interested in heading up something like that?"

I blink several times, trying to process the request. I was seriously thinking about this same thing several months ago, but the idea somehow got brushed off and forgotten about. A twinge of excitement bubbles in my stomach before it gets railroaded by a tidal wave of guilt and conviction.

I can go through the ritual of formatting and putting together a simple youth newsletter, filling in the blanks of a calendar with upcoming events, updating a Bible reading chart, and the whole works. But a *devotional*—something I'm supposed to write from my heart to inspire and encourage my peers or to offer them food for thought—is a different story.

If I didn't feel like a total fake before, I totally do now.

I know Anthony's waiting for an answer and probably wondering if my hesitation means I don't really want to do it and can't figure out how to tell him, but I honestly just don't know what to say. And I'm sure not going to tell him the *real* reason I'm not jumping on it. The truth is, I would've jumped on it just months ago, but now I feel unqualified.

"Well . . . I . . ." I'm struggling to find an answer.

Thankfully, Anthony chimes in. "You don't have to do it. I don't want you to feel pressured."

"No, it's fine. It's a great idea," I say, finally finding my voice. "I just, well, did you want me to start on it right away?"

My answer must've been the right one judging by the big smile on Anthony's face. Funny how I never noticed before what a great smile he has.

"That's awesome!" he says. "No, just think about it for a few weeks and jot some ideas down. We'll meet again and go over the details. I still need to put together a calendar of events for what we talked about in the meeting tonight."

"Sure, I can do that."

I wait for Anthony to stand up first because I'd be mortified if I stood up only to find out he had something more to say. Best to let him make the first move. But he just sits there, taking a sip of whatever's in his large black tumbler. It's one of those heavy-duty metal ones that could knock someone out if he swung it at their head.

Just as I scoot my chair back, he clears his throat and nods toward me. "That's a cool jacket."

Out of instinct, I glance down at my jean jacket, with the embroidered cuffs and frilled edges. It's not that I've forgotten what my favorite jacket looks like; I just need to look at it to see what Anthony sees that makes it so great.

Nope, nothing special. Just a jean jacket.

I look back up at him. "Oh, thanks." That's it.

I mean, what do I even say after that? Mention that I got it for my birthday last summer? Tell him his T-shirt looks great too? Which would be super weird because it's literally just a plain, gray T-shirt with a Nike logo blazed across the right side.

I stand. Maybe he still has stuff to work on and is waiting for me to pick up and leave. Maybe he feels awkward and just needs to say something, and that's why he complimented my jacket.

Suddenly, I'm more than ready to bow out of this meeting.

Anthony stands.

"So, I'll see you Wednesday night at Bible study," I mumble, pushing my chair in.

"Yeah, see you Wednesday." He starts collecting his notebook and tumbler. "You feeling better?"

I'm confused for a second. Then, my conscience pricks me when I realize that my family obviously told him I was "not feeling well" Friday night.

"Oh, yes, thank you. Much better."

Anthony comes around the table and walks with me toward the door, which I notice is no longer crowded in with bodies, but now empties into a vacated hallway. Realizing Anthony and I have been alone makes me feel self-conscious, like I used to feel hiding from my parents in the racks of the department store while they searched all over for me. It never ended well for me back then, so . . .

But Anthony and I aren't doing anything wrong.

Still, I don't want it to *look* bad. I slip past him into the hallway and wave while I march quickly toward the exit at the end of the hall. I push the door open with my shoulder and glance back to see Anthony looking my way as he locks the office door.

"Thanks again, Alli!" he says.

I nod, embarrassed that he caught me looking back at him, and let the door slam behind me.

Chapter Twenty-Four

"You guys look *so* cute together, Chad."

Shanice has such an endearing expression on her face that she almost looks pretty. Maybe she's always pretty, but I never notice because the only time she looks at me is when she's throwing dirty looks. I also love how she's talking about me and Chad but acting like I'm not here.

I start to pipe up with a "thanks," but Chad beats me to it as he slips his arm around me.

"Don't we, though?" He smiles down at me and winks.

It's the first time Chad's shown affection in front of others at school. Instead of feeling giddy with him openly claiming me as his girl, my stomach tightens, and my hands feel numb and tingly. It crosses my mind that I might be having my first anxiety attack.

I can't explain it, but for some reason, the idea of Chad and I being in a relationship felt safer when we were alone. Even at the party, he hadn't admitted to being an "item." Now, with

Shanice standing here, he doesn't deny the reality of our relationship. And I'm conflicted about how that makes me feel.

I'm irritated with myself for being so on the fence over this. Either I want it, or I don't. Sure, I'm infatuated with Chad, but our relationship hasn't ventured past the sensation of sitting close to a warm fire and enjoying its comforting benefits.

Out of nowhere, danger alarms blare in my mind from every direction as the flames of the fire I fanned over this relationship rush over me. Unpredictable flames that might get out of control before I know it. I want to run away, dance with joy, tell Chad to go away, give Chad a big hug . . . I couldn't be any more confused than I am right now.

Shanice finally looks at me and graces me with a big smile. One hundred percent fake—Shanice's trademark.

"Aw, how sweet." Her eyes lift back to Chad with an odd expression I can't quite discern. She looks almost, well, *amused.*

Is she wondering what he sees in me? I wonder. *Does Shanice have a thing for Chad?* If she does, that would explain why she has it out for me. "See you around, Chad," she says.

Glancing back at me as she turns, her parting remark is back to the Shanice I've come to know and detest.

"You should invite Chad to your church sometime, Alli, or maybe doll yourself up for him with a little makeup. You're looking a little pale." She winks before fluttering away.

"Man, I can't stand her," I mumble, but Chad doesn't seem to hear. His arm drops away as we walk to our next class.

～

I'M TOTALLY DRAGGING this morning as I get ready for school. Chad and I talked on the phone until one-thirty in the morning, and I've only had about four hours of sleep. I'm going to be a zombie in my classes today.

But it was worth it.

The more I'm around Chad, the more I'm attracted to him. He's so funny, and we never run out of things to talk about. Last night on the phone, he told me about his first summer camp when he was twelve and how his best friend lost his shorts swimming in the lake and was stuck in the water for hours until all the girl campers went in to get ready for dinner.

The way he told the story, painting the picture with his words, had me in stitches. I had to keep pushing a pillow against my face so no one else in the house would hear me laughing.

Chad even tried to get me to sneak out and meet him again, but there was no way I was going to attempt that with my whole family home. I'm not *that* brave. The last time I did that with Tessa, I was a nervous wreck.

But I *did* agree to meet him after school today and hang out for an hour or so before I go home. I plan to tell my mom that I'm going to study at the library for a while. She'll go for it because I stop by the library several times a month to pick up new books to read.

I slip on a cute floral dress and compliment it with a dark, denim vest. Grabbing my favorite brown sandals, I slip into the bathroom to brush my teeth and do something with my hair. I showered last night before bed, so that will save me some time.

I barely have enough time to spritz on some body spray and run out the door to make it to school before first period.

My mom waylays me in the kitchen before I make it out the door. "Alli, aren't you eating breakfast? I made waffles."

I *love* waffles. Especially my mom's two-inch thick, made-from-scratch waffles. But I don't have time this morning.

"Sorry, Mom. Running late. I gotta go."

She's already shoving two plain waffles into a sandwich bag. Then, she presses the air out of the bag and zips it up before handing it to me.

"At least eat these on the way. You need to have *something*."

I don't argue. Even plain and cold, they'll be amazing. "Thanks, Mom."

In true mom style, she leans over and kisses my cheek just as I slide past her to the door. "Have a great day at school," she says, making her way over to the coffee machine.

Popping my head back in the door, I act like I just remembered my plans. "Oh, yeah, Mom. I'm going to stop by the library for an hour or two after school, okay?"

She looks up from stirring creamer into her coffee and nods. "Alright. Be safe. Try to be home around six for dinner."

"Okay. See you!" I blow a kiss before racing down the sidewalk.

Well, that couldn't have gone any better.

Chapter Twenty-Five

BRYNNE ASKS me again today about having lunch together. I say louder than I need to that Chad and I already have plans to hang out. You know, just in case anyone's eavesdropping.

Chad and I have been getting some attention around campus. When we're together and someone stops to talk with Chad, they actually include me in the conversation now. I guess I feel validated by their attention.

It could also be my imagination, but I'm sure I've noticed jealous looks from other girls too. Chad's other friends—the jocks and cheerleaders, mostly—still pretend that I'm invisible and don't exist, but I don't care about them. I've even told Chad that I don't want to be anywhere near Shanice, Kim, or Tessa. I assume he knows Tessa and I used to be best friends, but he never asks for details.

But I feel bad for snubbing Brynne. She's been asking me all week, and the answer's been the same each day. You'd think she'd get the hint by now and let it rest, but she catches me in the hall as I'm leaving my last class of the day.

"Alli!"

I hear footsteps coming up behind me and I can tell they're coming fast. I don't bother turning around because I recognize the voice.

Be nice, Alli. Be nice . . .

She's out of breath when she pulls up beside me and matches my stride.

"Hey, Brynne," I say. "What's up?"

Taking another deep breath, she swallows. "Gosh, you're hard to keep up with," she says. "Do you want to come over to my house to work on our report?"

We're supposed to write a three-page research report on endangered primates for science. It's not the most exciting topic as it is, so I can't imagine it being any more interesting with a partner. Besides, I have plans with Chad right now, which she probably won't believe since I told her the same excuse for lunch today.

Maybe Brynne's never had a boyfriend and doesn't get it. That's what boyfriends and girlfriends do: they *hang out* with each other—like, every free moment they have.

I still feel a twinge of uncertainty about my relationship with Chad and where I stand with him. But with the way we talk, hang out, and hold hands, I just naturally assume that being a couple is how it is with us. We've even kissed a time or two during lunch and, last week, we met before school to go for a drive in his truck and ended up ditching first period.

"Sorry, girl. I can't. I'm meeting Chad in the parking lot

right now." I try to pull ahead, but she matches my stride again.

"Oh, gotcha. Well—"

I interrupt her before she bothers to ask about lunch or offer some other invitation I'll probably turn down. Stopping and turning to her, I say, "I have a lot going on this week, and Chad and I hang out most of the time, so I don't think we'd be able to work on the science project together."

By the look on Brynne's face, I think I've hit home.

"Alright. That's cool." She nods and turns away. "I'll catch you around."

I should be relieved to finally have her off my back, and I'm confident she won't be asking about lunch for a while, but I feel like a jerk. Brynne's cool to hang out with and we've had a lot of fun together lately. I have no reason to be so snappy with her. I should've found a nicer way to handle shaking her loose before catching up with Chad.

Speaking of Chad, he's probably sitting in his truck wondering what's holding me up. *I'll make it up to Brynne next weekend. Maybe invite her to spend the night and go shopping.*

I pick up the pace until I'm jogging out of the double doors leading to the back of the school, down the steps, and across the parking lot, where I find Chad leaning against his truck, scrolling through his cell phone.

"Sorry! Brynne stopped me in the hall . . ." I start to say, afraid he's irritated about making him wait. But when he looks up, he melts me with his bright smile, not a trace of irritation on his handsome face.

"No biggie. Let's go."

I sprint around to the passenger side and hop in. Chad

tosses his cell phone into the cup holder between us and reaches for my hand. My palm's sweaty from racing out to meet him, but he doesn't seem to notice.

Several students wave at us—actually, just at Chad—as we make our way out of the parking lot. I sneak a peek at Chad and study his handsome face with a few damp curls pressed against one of his cheeks. I have to turn away before he catches me staring.

"Man, we had a sub in fourth period today that was something out of a nightmare," I say. "And I thought Mr. O was strict."

Mr. O'Malley, Mr. O for short, is my fourth-period algebra teacher. It's bad enough that I detest math in any form—algebra ranking near the top—but it makes it worse that Mr. O is perpetually irritated and freaks me out. I would just as soon pour boiling water over myself than ask him for help.

"I had a headache for an hour after this guy," I continue. "All he did was stand in the front of the room and yell at us the whole time. Jayden made the fatal mistake of telling him that we didn't understand the instructions on the worksheet Mr. O left for us to do, and the guy lost it. I mean, seriously, I had no clue on how to do the worksheet. Sure hope Mr. O isn't giving us a grade on it."

I realize that I'm blabbing on and on, but Chad seems distracted. I stop talking and wait to see if he picks up the conversation.

He looks over when he finally notices that I've gone quiet. "You gonna give Mr. O a big hug to welcome him back tomorrow?" He winks, and I laugh.

"I should."

We head left instead of my usual right out of the parking lot and make our way toward the south of town. Chad and I had talked about what we wanted to do after school and agreed to grab some fast food, go to the park, and have an impromptu picnic—minus the cozy basket with a checkered cloth or even a blanket for the occasion. But I'm still determined to have a good time.

There's a huge pond in the park that has several benches where we can sit and feed the ducks. I could tell Chad wasn't super excited about the idea when I mentioned it, but we didn't have many options to choose from since I only have an hour or two before I need to be home.

After driving for five minutes, Chad pulls into a gas station and steers the truck next to a pump. "I gotta grab gas really quick," he says, shutting the engine off. "I only have cash, so I have to run in. Be right back."

He hops out of the truck, then leans back in to grab his wallet from his jacket pocket on the back of his seat. "You want anything?"

"Nah, I'm good."

I watch him walk down the sidewalk to the front of the store, swaying like a New York runway model, self-assured and with a healthy dose of ego in his strut. With a quick flip of his hair, he's through the glass doors and out of my sight.

I sigh. *How did I get so lucky?*

Knowing it's probably pointless, I poke my head in the backseat to see if there's anything we could sit on at the park. Chad must be a neat freak because there isn't so much as an old

French fry or anything laying around in the back besides his backpack.

Settling back against my seat, I look down and notice Chad's cell phone is still sitting in the cupholder. I glance up at the front of the store, but there's no sign of him.

I look back at his phone and rest my hand on top of it. I can't believe what I'm considering doing, but curiosity urges me on.

Just a quick look. Go on, pick it up.

I slide the phone onto my lap and turn it over. I don't know his password, but not everyone uses one. I'm hoping it's unlocked, and I can just peek at the photos on his phone. I don't even know what I'm expecting to find. Pictures of an old girlfriend? Family photos that'll give me insight into his personal life?

But before I even tap on anything, a notification pops up on his lock screen. The message is from someone named Kim. I only know of one Kim at our high school who would have Chad's number, but the name's a common one. He could even have a cousin or—

Where u at? I thought u were going to Brad's? Don't tell me ur with your hot girlfriend? Lol. Seriously, Chad. Just tell her and move on already. She's gonna find out the truth sooner or later anyway.

The words on the screen—glaring up at me like a neon sign —suck all the air from my lungs.

My eyes sting, and I blink several times to clear the blurriness that comes out of nowhere. I look up, see that Chad's on his way back, look back down at the notification, then throw the phone on Chad's seat. I don't stop to sort through all the fireworks exploding in my head.

Wait. Stop. Think, Alli! Don't overreact.

My skull feels like a grenade detonated inside it, and the need to run hijacks my limbs as I snatch up my purse and fling open the passenger door. I slam the door closed just as Chad opens his, and I see his confused expression when I pass him as I run toward the street. His mouth moves, but I can't hear what he's saying.

I'm halfway through the parking lot when I hear Chad calling my name. I glance over my shoulder to see him standing outside of his truck, phone in hand. He's obviously seen the same text I just saw.

"Alli! Wait! It's not what you think!" he calls again.

Jerking around to face him, I hold my hand out to warn him not to come any closer.

"Oh, what am I *thinking*, Chad? That you used me in some cruel, freak prank for . . .for *what*? To give Kim and Shanice a good laugh? For your football buddies? For something cool to post on social media—prank of the year? I hate you. All of you."

My chest feels heavy, and I know I'm about to lose it. I don't wait for his answer. I spin around and start walking. I can't even stand to look at him right now.

"I know it was wrong, Alli," Chad says, "but I was going to talk to you about it today. It's not like that now. I think you're a great girl—"

"Stay away from me, Chad!" I scream and break into a run,

hoping he isn't following me because I don't know what I'll do if he is.

There's another gas station on the next block and I instinctively head for it, wanting to reach another public place away from him where I can pull out my cell phone and call for someone—anyone—to come and get me.

I don't care if my mom wonders why I'm at a gas station miles away from the library, where I'm supposed to be. I'll take a month of restriction and every lecture my parents can throw at me over what I just read.

She's gonna find out the truth sooner or later anyway.

Kim. Cheer captain, Kim.

The details fit together too seamlessly for me to be wrong.

I race through the brush on the side of the road, not caring that dry branches tear at my bare legs and hot tears stream down my face. Someone driving past might worry that I'm being chased by an abductor the way I'm running, but I couldn't care less.

With a quick glance at the road and my ears tuned for Chad's truck, I don't slow down until I see the other gas station in sight.

It isn't until I finally stop and crouch behind a telephone pole on the street corner that I realize Chad isn't coming for me. More than likely, he's sitting in his truck, already on the phone with Kim, telling her how she should've seen my face, how stupid I'd been to not see it sooner, and … whatever else my imagination conjures up, which brings on a fresh round of tears of mortification.

I decide to wait it out a few minutes just in case Chad does end up coming back this way. I don't think I could suffer any more humiliation right now, so I don't want him seeing me hiding like a runaway behind a concrete pole, with leaves and branches stuck on my clothes and in my hair and a blotchy, tear-streaked face. With my luck, he'd probably snap a picture of me with his cell phone for a grand finale of the perfect hoax.

Seriously, Chad. Just tell her and move on already.

Why would you do this to me, Chad?

I breathe deeply, trying to still the quaking in my chest and calm myself before I attempt to call my mom and freak her out. Then, I hear an engine approaching the stop sign behind me, and I freeze. I jerk my chin in the air in a feeble display of courage just in case it's him, but the vehicle moves on and I see it's just an old, blue sedan making its way down the road.

Still, I'm not ready to move yet. It's like my body refuses to move until I make sense of what happened back there.

Why would Chad mess with me that way? How long was Kim in on all this?

I think of Shanice's syrupy smile when she saw Chad and me together.

What was the point? Is this just another sadistic head game the in-crowd does to get their thrills? I should've known Shanice and Kim would be part of this.

Cheerleaders.

Tessa.

No way! Tessa's in on this. I just know it!

Was this her idea? Her initiation into the popular crowd? Make a fool of her insignificant ex-best friend to show that she's worthy enough to rub shoulders with the higher class? How could she?

I would start bawling again if I weren't paralyzed with shock and anger at the thought of Tessa stooping so low. I'm more dumbstruck by the thought of *Why would Tessa do this?* than I am with *Why would Chad do this?*

Both are devastating blows, but Tessa's knife cuts way deeper than Chad's. I didn't grow up with Chad as my best friend.

Sheer adrenaline drives me across the street—I'm almost daring Chad to show up at this point—to the gas station and through its front door, where I spot a restroom sign near the rear of the store. I'm glad to see that it's a single-occupant bathroom and waste no time pushing the slider lock into place and plunking myself down on the lid of the toilet seat.

I won't cry. I won't cry.

Somewhere between the telephone pole and the first set of gas pumps, I decided I wouldn't call my mom or anyone else for a ride; I'd walk home. I'm only about two or three miles from my house and can make it back within an hour, still within the time range my mom would be expecting me home from the library.

But I'll have to clean myself up before I leave the gas station so I don't look like I ran through a forest of bramble bushes—which is exactly what I've done. That way, I won't have to deal with my mom's emotional breakdown when I'm going through my own right now.

Even though I'd resolved not to, I start to cry.

Chapter Twenty-Six

"You *KNEW*! How could you—"

"Alli, I promise! I had no idea Kim and Shanice were behind this."

I'm almost spitting in Tessa's face, seething with uncontrollable anger, humiliation, and a mountain of other emotions that overwhelm me as I glare at her.

"You're a liar, Tessa. It's bad enough that you discarded our friendship like a worthless bag of trash on the side of the road, but I never thought you would stoop this low. What did I ever do to you? Why do you have it out for me?"

I made record time walking home from the gas station—probably because I was so wound up and walked with the stride of a maniac—so I took the extra time to make a detour by Tessa's house to see if she was there.

She was.

When I got there, I sent her a text telling her I needed to talk with her outside for a minute. I didn't *ask*; I *told*. Then, when she stepped out on her front porch in bright pink sweat-pants and an oversized SeaWorld T-shirt, with her hair pulled up into a messy bun, I didn't give her time to ask questions.

Every humiliation and degrading comment I'd endured over the past few months, ending with the one that knocked the breath out of me today, came flooding out past the broken dam that was holding it all in check until now.

Tessa's eyes grew wider the more I unleashed everything I needed to say. And when I dropped the revelation of how I discovered the text message on Chad's phone and started to piece it all together, her eyes were the size of saucers.

That's when she tried to deny it.

"Right, Tessa."

I throw in a drastic hand wave to emphasize my dramatic eye roll. "You had *no* idea what Kim and Shanice were up to, which I think is especially interesting since you brought Shanice's name up when I only mentioned Kim's. And all this after you acted like you were trying to warn me away from Chad at the party. Do I have the word *stupid* written across my forehead?"

"I brought up Shanice because anything Kim's involved in is almost always Shanice's idea. Kim doesn't think of this kind of stuff on her own. Not something this well planned out," Tessa says, her eyes glistening with unshed tears that do nothing to move me to have sympathy.

"Listen," she says, "I knew something was off because Kim and Shanice hang out with Chad, and they were too laid back about him showing interest in you suddenly. I mean, normally they'd be all over Chad for even looking your way.

No offense, but it's obvious Chad's crowd isn't the kind you hang with—"

"Oh, but *you* hang with that crowd?" I fire back.

The old Tessa would've snapped back at me, but she seems genuinely upset, unless she's become a skilled actress all of a sudden. The latter seems more likely, especially since I hardly know this new version of Tessa.

"You know what I mean, Alli," she says. "Didn't you think it was weird that Chad started coming on to you when he never even gave you the time of day before?"

That hits me hard. I don't know why either, because she's right. I *did* ignore all the warning signs, drunk with the idea that a good-looking, popular jock from school would treat me like an equal candidate for his affection against the flawless skin and perfect bodies of the popular girls he could pick from any time he wanted.

What's left of my boiling rage drains out, leaving me a deflated balloon of emotions, but I keep it in check in front of Tessa. I'm desperate to keep some measure of pride to cling to while the picture of how I've been played the fool has been obvious to everyone but me.

Good old, Alli. Always late to the show.

I decide not to answer Tessa's question. The answer would be a yes, but I'm not ready to admit it.

"I know you don't believe me, Alli, but I had no idea that this was a setup and that they were pranking you. I've known all along that Chad is a player. That's what I tried to warn you about at the party. You just didn't want to hear it." She sighs. "I know we haven't exactly been close lately, but I would never pull something so vicious. Honest, Alli."

Tessa's expression shifts subtly from prey to predator.

"Since you decided to show up and give me a piece of your mind—which I totally don't deserve, whether you want to believe it or not—then I'm gonna give it right back to you. What were you even doing at the party that night, Alli? What's going on with you?"

Despite the shock of her words, I don't let her off that easy. "Don't try to turn this away from you and onto me, Tessa. I didn't come here to talk about me. It's none of your business what I do with my life since you aren't part of it anymore. You're the one who went your own way, thinking you're better off with your new friends instead of me. And now you expect me to believe you were clueless that your friends were messing with me."

Tessa had been leaning back against the front door jam, but now she pushes off and jumps in my face.

"Oh, don't even go there, Alli. I thought you said you came here to talk about the Chad business, and now you're bringing our friendship up? It's so hypocritical of you to criticize my choice of friends when you shut me down about why you were at that party—which is technically *my* turf and *my* friends. Using your own words, 'It's none of your business what I do with my life.'"

I can see this conversation is going nowhere, and I begin to wonder why I even came here. The more I think about it, the more I worry that all I've accomplished here today is giving Tessa something else to talk about with her friends.

"Tessa? Alli? Everything okay out here?"

Mrs. Williams stands behind the screen door peering out at us. I don't want her to know that Tessa and I are currently throwing poison darts at each other. Of course, I have no idea what Tessa's already shared with her about us and our friendship.

I plaster on a smile. "Hi, Mrs. Williams." I leave it at that. I'll let Tessa take it from here.

Tessa leans back on the door jamb, glaring at me, but her voice is soft when she answers. "We're good, Mom."

Mrs. Williams is wearing a bathrobe, and her hair is a tangled mess. In all the years I've known her, I've never seen Tessa's mom in a bathrobe before bedtime. She's always been so put together.

"Hi, sweety." Mrs. Williams' voice isn't chipper and friendly like it usually is. She's always been bouncy and cheerful with plenty of energy to keep up with Tessa and me even during our crazy, over-caffeinated, late-night sleepovers.

I half expect her to shove the door open and wave me into the house because she has a batch of cookies she just baked that I just *have* to come in and sample.

But she doesn't do that. And—despite the rage I'm harboring toward Tessa—my curiosity is stirred.

What's wrong with Tessa's mom?

"Well, it's nice to see you, Alli. We've been missing you," Mrs. Williams says. "Tessa, don't forget to take the trash out, okay?"

I can feel Tessa still looking at me, but my eyes are pinned to the doorway from where Mrs. Williams just retreated. A wave of recent memories comes flooding forward. Stuff Tessa and I had talked about before she drifted to the dark side. Stuff about her family . . . and how her parents were getting a divorce.

My attention pulls back to Tessa. I forget the huge gulf separating us and our differences and feel an old thread of connection lingering.

"Are they still going through with the divorce?"

Tessa doesn't answer for a moment, and I wonder if she will. Just because I still feel the connection regardless of everything we just vomited on each other, doesn't mean Tessa feels it.

"Dad's been gone. You knew that. And, yeah, the divorce is still in the works." Her expression is still angry and hard, but there's a weary look in her eyes that I hadn't noticed before.

It's like someone sucker-punches me in the gut, and I have a hard time catching my breath. I feel like it's my own family falling apart. The drama between us and the whole Chad deal fades to the background as I blink back the tears.

Tessa looks away, staring past the porch and up into the sky somewhere. Anywhere but at me.

"Gosh, I'm sorry, Tessa."

She shrugs. "Happens to lots of families."

I start to reach out just to offer a touch of comfort, but she stiffens and turns toward the door, dismissing me.

But I don't retreat just yet. "If you ever need someone to talk to . . ."

Opening the screen door, she looks over her shoulder. "I'm a big girl, Alli. I'm handling it just fine."

Yeah, Tessa, I think. *I can see how well you've been handling it with all the choices you've been making.*

I turn to leave. Then, I hear Tessa call my name from the other side of the screen door.

I turn back.

"I was telling the truth about not knowing what Kim and Shanice were up to," she says.

I stare at Tessa through the haze of mesh that separates us and nod.

"Thanks."

Chapter Twenty-Seven

I WAIT the whole morning in misery, hoping for Chad to come running up to say how sorry he was. That it was all a misunderstanding. That the text I saw wasn't what I thought it was.

But that doesn't happen.

Maybe that was what Chad was trying to tell me when I ran away from him in the parking lot. *Should I have stopped and heard him out?*

I almost let my heart go there but stop myself before I do. Even if Chad *did* try to tell me that it was a misunderstanding, I would know it was a lie. The truth was right there staring up at me from the text on his phone.

I doubt Chad will make any effort at this point, anyway. Why would he? The deed is done. There's no need to fake it anymore. I mean, he *does* have my number, and I didn't get any calls or texts from him last night. The only notification I got on my phone this morning was my blaring alarm prodding me to get up and get ready for school.

My stomach is in knots. If I had high blood pressure, I'm positive it would feel exactly like I'm feeling right now, with my heart pumping as if it's trying to push sludge through a straw and with the sound of a waterfall rushing through my eardrums.

I haven't seen Chad all morning, and he knows exactly where to find me.

At the same time, I'm petrified that he will.

What would I say to Chad if we ran into each other? Would he act like he doesn't know I exist just like before he started messing with me? And that's what he did, plain and simple: messed with me. Like a yo-yo that he just bounced around to distract him from boredom. Or was it a dare from his friends to see how far he could string me along? The higher he made me feel, the harder I would fall, right?

Chad and I don't have any classes together, which is something I was bummed about before but now consider a blessing. But I do have Tessa in science and Shanice in a couple classes. And, although Tessa's gracious enough to not even look my way (*how generous of her*), Shanice makes it a point to smirk and giggle whenever she catches my eye.

I wish I could slap the smile off her face, but I would never have the guts to do it, and I don't need any extra attention on me right now. Nor do I want to act like all this bothers me, but you'd have to have your head in the clouds to believe it doesn't. Everyone in the whole school saw Chad and me together, and it was obvious we weren't just casual acquaintances. I look like a fool now.

I purposely avoid Maribel in journalism, acting like I'm totally engrossed in the teen risk-taking article I've been working on while keeping one eye peeled for her hallmark black curls. It's the last class period and I don't need to end my day with her gloating over my downfall. I can just hear her now: "If you'd have just let *me* do that interview with Chad, none of this would've happened."

When the bell rings, I linger in my seat a minute longer so I don't have to talk to anyone. I've never been so grateful for my mom picking me up after school for a doctor's appointment. She arrives on time too, so I hustle out the doors and into the car without any uncomfortable intrusions.

When I slam the door and turn to throw my backpack in the back seat, my mom stares at me with one eyebrow raised.

"Someone's in a hurry," she says. "I've never seen you so excited about going to a doctor's appointment."

I roll my eyes, trying to play off my over-ambitious entrance. "I'm just glad to get out of here. It was the longest day ever."

She puts the car into gear and pulls away from the curb. "Aw, sorry, hon. Do you want to—"

"No, I don't. Can we stop at Starbucks after my appointment?" I quickly steer the topic in a new direction.

She gives me another eyebrow raise before giving the road her full attention. "Sure . . . that sounds okay . . . I guess." There's hesitancy in her voice, but she doesn't push. "I think I still have a balance on my gift card."

I TURNED my article about teen risk-taking over to Scott this morning. I wonder if he'll be able to read between the lines about how personal the article is for me. As in *Tessa* personal.

Yeah, I wrote about Tessa. No, her name wasn't mentioned, and you wouldn't know it's about her unless you "read between the lines."

Tessa's been making a mess of her life. She's so wrapped up with being part of the inner circle crowd that she compromises more and more of the real Tessa to become a counterfeit version. From what I overhear in first period, she goes to all the exclusive parties—the parties she and I used to sneak out of the house to go watch from the bushes, the outsiders wanting to be in.

Now, Tessa's in, and I'm still an outsider. I tell myself every day that it doesn't matter, but I can't deny that my heart still feels it.

I'm not spying on Tessa. But it just so happens that Avery parades into my room most nights with news from her friend whose sister's on the cheer team. Apparently, her friend sits outside her sister's bedroom door and listens to her conversations. Plus, I think Avery's made it her personal mission to validate me by finding dirt on Tessa and reporting it back to me. I act like I don't care, but I don't tell her to stop either.

Tessa's always off on some trip to games where she's cheering. I notice she obviously got the money for her new uniform and all the accessories she needs. She's been sporting designer purses and clothes too, and I can't help but feel curious about where she's getting all the cash for that since her family's never had the money for that kind of excess before. Maybe her parents *are* buying her new stuff out of guilt over the divorce, or maybe they're trying to compete for favor with Tessa and Aaron.

And now there are other rumors. Not just from Avery and her little spy friend either.

Jennifer, one of the girls who has a locker close to mine, told me the other day that she overheard some girls say Tessa might be pregnant. She didn't catch any of the guys' names who Tessa could've been involved with, but she said the girls talking about it seemed confident about their information. I've never seen Tessa with just one guy at school who could be a boyfriend or anything. Was it a one-night stand? Did she even know him very well?

When I first heard it, I didn't know whether to believe it or not, but I wouldn't be totally surprised if it is true, given the crowd she hangs with these days. Still, no matter how wicked Tessa's been toward me, I refused to comment and chose to ignore the gossip.

Then, I got a call from Tessa last night. I don't know if I'm more stunned that she dared to reach out to me or shocked that I'm still on the list of people she trusts.

We talked for over an hour. Well, *she* talked and cried, and *I* listened. It was better that way since I was mute with shock and couldn't process what she was telling me at first anyway.

"How am I going to tell my parents? I can't deal with a *baby* in my life right now!" she wailed.

I honestly didn't know what to say. I was as shell-shocked

as she was. But when I found my voice again, I tried to help her think of ways to talk to her mom and dad, and I bravely asked her if the guy she was with even knew yet (I didn't ask *who*).

She said he didn't. This brought on a whole new flood of tears. "I'm not telling him," she said between hiccups. "No way."

"Tessa. You *have* to tell him. He has the right to know. If he walks away, well, then you at least tried." I lower my voice. "You could have the baby and give it up for adoption."

She couldn't even answer. I just listened to her sob for several minutes before she pulled herself together.

"You're right, Alli," she said after a while. "I just need some time to think of how to handle this."

After talking for a few more minutes, she said she needed to go because her mom had called her three times, and she needed to wash her face so her mom wouldn't know she'd been crying.

"Thanks, Alli. I know you're probably wondering why I called you, but you were the only person that I could think of that would know what to do and . . ." she hesitated, "wouldn't judge me. And I knew you would pray for me."

My heart lifted to hear that she recalled some redeeming qualities from our past friendship. "I appreciate your honesty," I said. "It's just that . . . wow, I don't know what to say, Tessa, but I'm glad you called. It's not going to be easy, but everything will be okay. You can do this."

"I know. I'm going to *have* to. It's not like I have many choices left about anything these days." She sniffed. "I'll call you tomorrow maybe? If you don't mind, that is."

I let myself smile. "I don't mind. For what it's worth, I'm here for you."

You did have a choice, Tessa, I thought. But it's useless to voice it now.

TESSA NEVER CALLS.

I try to call her once or twice during the week but end up getting her voicemail. I only leave a message the first time, reminding her that I'm praying for her and that I hope she's alright.

I don't have the guts to approach her at school. Not with her shadowing Kim and Shanice everywhere.

Even though Tessa laughs and chats it up with her friends, I can't imagine what she's struggling with inside. Tessa's always been good at hiding things. But I know her better than she probably thinks I do. I can't help but wonder if she cries at night, if her parents know, or if she's even told the baby daddy yet. It's obvious Tessa won't be able to hide her pregnancy for long.

Maybe she hasn't called me back because she's embarrassed or thinks I'm judging her for getting herself in this mess. I try to catch her eye when I pass her in class or in the hallway, but she avoids me like I have a contagious disease.

Does she think I would condemn her because of my faith? I mean, I've never made her feel that way before, and we've done some not-so-angelic stuff together plenty of times. It makes me wonder what she was thinking of *me* when I was doe-eyed and infatuated with Chad even after she tried to warn me about his character.

I stoop so low as to ask Avery if her friend has overhead anything new from her sister about Tessa or her friends. I don't offer any hints about Tessa's secret but try to make it seem like I'm just being nosy.

Avery assures me she hasn't heard a thing.

I wrestle with the seriousness of the situation and wonder if I should tell an adult, but Tessa would hate me forever if I did that. And when I almost convince myself that I should do it anyway—that it's the right thing to do—a voice reminds me that Tessa has dirt on me too and could throw me under the bus just as fast.

So, I do what I think Tessa would want me to do. Nothing.

Except pray. She would expect that—*want* that.

And I'm not even doing that great with that simple expectation. Because I'm still living with that dirt Tessa has on me.

Yeah, I go to church. I clap my hands with the music and nod my head with the preaching. I shake hands after service and say all the right things at all the right times and stay involved with youth activities and the youth planning committee. But I don't *feel* anything when I do all that stuff.

Is that a dangerous place to be?

I don't know how I ended up stuck in this hamster wheel of self-doubt—if you don't count all the stupid decisions I've made over the past few months and the fact that I've stuck my big toe over several lines I would never have dreamed of crossing months ago.

I've heard at least a hundred times over the pulpit and in

youth services about how God knows our weaknesses, understands our struggles, and is always ready and willing to forgive. I believe it all. I really do. And I love God. But I sense myself resisting him and wanting to do my own thing. It's like I'm restless and tired of being the good girl who follows the rules all the time. But the thing is, I don't feel okay about *breaking* the rules either.

My dad told me once that our relationship with God shouldn't feel like a drudgery of mandates to follow but that it should be a choice of love. In my heart, I know I love God, so why does submitting to His plan seem so hard?

There's a scripture in the Bible that talks about our humanity always being at war with our spirit. Right now, I'm losing the battle to the wrong side.

I haven't always been the best example to Tessa of what my faith means to me, but I've tried. And I believe Tessa saw that. She would always tell me that she knew she wasn't the best influence for me, and maybe she was right on some points. She *has* always been so persuasive in talking me into running off to mischief with her, but not once was I able to talk her into coming to church with me. Maybe I've been losing the battle for a long time and just didn't know it.

Now Tessa's in serious trouble, and I still don't have even a small bit of influence over her for the good. She's surrounded by worldly friends, buffeted with conflicting morals, and influenced by things that will only end up destroying her if she doesn't rise above it all.

Who am I to judge?

But Tessa called *me* looking for help. By her own admission, she said she didn't know what to do. How can Tessa over-come that without help? If her mom's as bad off as she looked the day I dropped in on Tessa, I can't imagine how she endured hearing that her only daughter is pregnant at seventeen—if Tessa's even told her yet.

All the anger and bitterness against Tessa I've stewed on lately pales in comparison to how disappointed I am in myself for failing her as a friend. I should've taken the higher ground and shown Tessa love, instead of obsessing over taking vengeance and casting blame. And I'm ashamed to admit that praying for Tessa has not been my priority.

Could my prayers have helped?

Chapter Twenty-Eight

S HANICE DIDN'T COME to school today, so I finally have a chance to get Tessa alone as we file out of science class. She scoots toward the door, but I'm faster and time it just right.

"Hey, Tessa." I take a quick breath. "How come you haven't called me back?" I hadn't planned to pounce on her with that opening, but our time's limited.

Tessa gives me a timid smile and looks away but not before I notice the haunted look in her eyes. "Sorry," she says. "I've been meaning to, but it was never the right time. Plus, I've had a lot going on."

She picks up the pace and pulls ahead. But I'm determined to keep up. "Why didn't you at least text me? I was waiting—"

When she stops, our shoulders collide. Tessa turns around, and our eyes meet.

I finally have her full attention.

"I should've sent a text or called, Alli. I'm sorry. It's just that . . . well, I thought it wouldn't go well."

Her eyes drop to the floor. "I . . . know what you *really* want to know. It's why I've been avoiding you. I know you see things differently than I do. But I . . . I took care of it, Alli. Everything's fine now."

The world stops so suddenly that it jolts me to the core as I stare at her in shock. Someone bumps against my backpack as they pass, but I hardly notice. The only living, breathing bodies that exist right now in this crowded hallway are me and Tessa. I don't want to ask the question—don't even *need* to ask the question—but I still feel compelled to say *something*.

"What do you mean, 'took care of it,' Tessa?" My bottom lip trembles and my eyes start to burn. My stomach threatens to unload breakfast at my feet.

I can see that Tessa's struggling too. She pales and shakes her head, looks down, then back up to me, then brings her fist to her lips—a physical dam to restrain all the emotions that I can tell threaten to spill out of her.

When Tessa shifts her gaze back on me, the pain in her eyes is so deep and raw that it almost paralyzes me. I wonder if this is what it's like to look into the eyes of a dying man.

"*How*? Please don't tell me—" I start, fumbling with the words. "Who was in on this, Tessa? Did Shanice . . ."

Her eyes well with tears that threaten to overflow, but she blinks them away, refusing to let them fall or even to acknowledge their existence. When Tessa takes a step back, I know I'm losing her.

"Tessa?" I try to call her back to me, a thousand words on my tongue that I want to say to reassure her that I'm still here, that I'm hurting with her. But . . .

Tessa's fist snaps open, her palm blocking my face and stopping me from coming closer, as if she can't bear to hear what I have to say or see her own pain reflected in my eyes.

"I can't . . . I don't want to talk about it, Alli. It's over. Done." Her hand waves in the air as if she's attempting to erase the bitter memory of it all. She looks away and bites hard on her bottom lip. "I have to go."

She leaves me standing in the middle of the now-empty hallway. I know I'm late for a class, but for the life of me, I can't remember where I'm supposed to be.

I FEEL the tap on my shoulder, and then something rubs against my right elbow. I glance down and see a white paper folded into a neat square. Glancing up to make sure Mr. Foster, our economics teacher, isn't looking, I tug it from Brynne's fingers and rest it on my lap.

Careful not to crinkle the paper too loudly, I open the note.

ARE YOU OK?

The words are written in big, block letters with a pink marker. I refold the note and tuck it in my pocket. It would be more obvious if I tried to pass a note back to her since I would have to turn around in my seat. Instead, I glance sideways and give her a nod. I can catch up with her after class.

Somehow, I made it through third and fourth period, though I couldn't tell you what we did in either class. Now, in fifth period, the fog is barely lifting, and I know I've got to get it together, or I'll have a lot of catching up to do with my class-work later.

As soon as the bell rings, I turn to Brynne.

"Hey," I say. "Ready for the test tomorrow?"

"I'm never ready for any of the tests in this class," she huffs. "Do you have any gum?"

I shrug my backpack off my shoulder onto the chair and dig out some gum. Brynne thanks me and we walk to our next class together. Her American history class is next to my journalism class.

Brynne eyes me as we walk. She's trying hard not to be obvious, which makes her more . . . obvious.

"So . . . what's going on?" she finally asks.

Brynne observed the whole Chad ordeal from a distance, watching us go everywhere together around campus, including sneaking off to our special lunch spot—which I now avoid with all its bad vibes—having me turn down her invites to hang out, and then noticing me being solo again.

She never asked, but I'm almost positive everyone at school was talking about our breakup *(more like the grand finale of the Chad's Prank of the Year show)* and probably adding their own twist or beefing up the drama just for the sake of having something to talk about.

I basically existed in a fog for a week or two after the Chad ordeal, just trying to stay under the radar and bear the humiliation the best I could. Now, just when I'm starting to see the light again, Tessa's news casts another dark cloud over me.

If Brynne only knew what's really weighing on my heart, I think.

I've noticed Brynne seems to go out of her way to be nice lately and tries to distract me in science by teasing Zach and complaining more than usual about the labs and endless notes we have to write.

A people-pleaser myself, I would usually put on a smile and attempt to look like I'm over whatever had upset my universe even when I don't feel like it, but I wasn't having it those couple of weeks. I would've preferred to crawl under a desk and stay there every day if I could have, but I couldn't chance a truancy call home to my parents.

I'm guessing Brynne wants the full scoop to bring her up to date, not just the reason why I seem extra distracted today. But I'm not ready to talk about Chad. I probably won't feel like talking about Chad or a whole lot of things for a long time.

And, as for what's bothering me more than any drama that'll fade with the list of other bad high school memories—the thing that'll more than likely haunt me the rest of my life—I'm *definitely* not going to talk about that with Brynne.

Still, she deserves something for her patience and quiet persistence at trying to be a friend to me.

I sigh and lower my voice as we pass a group of guys standing outside Brynne's class. "I'm sure you already know part of what's been bothering me lately. And, not to be rude, I don't even want to go there right now. But I also got some bad news today and I'm just trying to process it." I shrug, knowing my attempt at an explanation was lame, at best.

Brynne nods and leans in for a quick side hug. "Aw, I'm sorry, Alli. Are you gonna be okay?"

"I think so." *Not for a while, though.*

"If you ever need to talk, I'm here." She smiles and gives me a small wave before she turns to go.

I manage a small wave back.

Funny how that small effort makes my world feel a little better.

Chapter Twenty-Nine

It's not often that I don't have a phone or some other electronic device in my hands, but I guess this is one of those not-often moments as I sit on the back porch drinking coffee.

Yeah, sounds like something an old granny would do, right? But believe it or not, I like to sit out here occasionally, and just think about stuff. It doesn't even have to be deep, serious thoughts. I can just sit and listen to the birds, lawnmowers, barking dogs, or my neighbor's collection of wind chimes.

You know, normal, everyday, boring *stuff*.

As a matter of fact, I used to do this very thing with my old granny. Well, she wasn't all *that* old, depending on what you consider *old*. Anyway, sitting on the porch drinking coffee makes me feel warm fuzzies because it reminds me of Nonna Mancini, my dad's mother.

When Nonna would come out to visit, she would always

say to me, "Allisandra," (Nonna always called me by my full name), "come sit with me on the porch."

It was one of my favorite things to do with her because it was one of those rare moments when I got Nonna all to myself. No interruptions. No other adults around to pull her attention away. I could talk about whatever I wanted, and Nonna never interrupted or scolded me. She was one of the only adults in my life who gave me their undivided attention, outside of my parents and teachers constantly scolding or lecturing me.

And I loved her for it.

Nonna would fix herself a cup of coffee and carry it to the back porch. As we sat on the cushioned porch chairs, Nonna would nod and say, "Is that right?" as I chattered away about whatever topic interested me during that phase in my life.

One time, it was about how I was planning to become a professional skateboarder, and Nonna asked detailed questions about the best types of skateboards for doing the tricks I tried to describe for her. Another phase was me going on and on about the hot new boy band all the girls fell all over themselves about. I didn't even listen to their music or know any of the band's songs, but I wanted to sound cool for my nonna. She was easy to impress, and I desperately needed that boost to my ego.

There were also plenty of times I shared how I was struggling in my classes, how my parents didn't understand me, and even how I felt gross because my face had broken out with another wave of acne.

Nonna would pass her coffee to me and let me take sips. It was another way she endeared me to her since my mom insisted

I wasn't allowed to drink coffee until I was older because she didn't want me to get addicted to caffeine. If my mom only knew what some of the kids I went to school with were doing and addicted to, a caffeine addiction would be the least of her worries.

A small, brown sparrow swoops onto the porch step while I reminisce, and I smile as I watch it hop around and flutter its wings. Another bird I can't identify squawks its head off in the branches above the roof, and I wonder what he's going on about. Then, I wonder why I even care about random birds. Then again, I wish that was the only thing I was wondering about in life right now.

"I miss you, Nonna."

The brown sparrow startles at the sound of my voice and takes flight. "Sorry, little guy."

I take a sip of my coffee, which is now growing cold—and I hate cold coffee. But the bitter taste of it mingled with the overkill of creamer brings back fond memories, and I brave another sip. Who knew that a lukewarm cup of coffee could calm all the anxiety in my head, which feels like a hundred volcanoes erupting, one after another?

What I wouldn't give to be sitting here with Nonna right now, pouring out my problems, which have escalated since the days of face breakouts and skateboard choices.

KRISTIN CATCHES my eye above several heads and jabs a finger excitedly toward my left as she makes her way through the crowd between us. Her face glows with anticipation—or exertion. Maybe both.

My head bobs, my eyes darting to the person next to me while trying not to make it obvious. I grin like a drunk hyena, mouthing the words to Kristin when her head resurfaces above the crowd: *She's here.*

After getting ambushed by the Fletcher twins, who beg Kristin for candy they know she keeps in her purse, and hijacked by Sister Vance, an elderly lady in the church who can talk for hours if you don't find a creative way to shake her off, Kristin finally reaches me just as Brynne does.

Kristin steps forward and welcomes her with a beaming smile and friendly handshake.

"Hey, Brynne. I'm Kristin. It's great to meet you. I'm glad you made it tonight," she says.

Brynne smiles back but looks confused by the handshake thing. Everyone shakes hands at church. I've never thought much about it, having grown up in church, but I guess not everyone is used to it like I am. Brynne holds up a limp hand, and Kristin takes it with a firm shake.

"Yeah, it's good to meet you too," Brynne says.

Kristin and I lead the way to youth class with Brynne sandwiched between us. We look like two guards escorting a dangerous inmate with the way we hover close to her. Our closeness also helps to block Sister Vance's view of Brynne, so she doesn't make her way over. We'd never make it to youth class if she did.

Several of the youth members greet us as we come in, and they go out of their way to make Brynne feel welcome. I've never really noticed before what a friendly group we have, and it makes me proud.

"Where are we supposed to sit?" Brynne whispers. She's pressed close to me like she's afraid to let me out of her sight.

"Wherever we want," I whisper back. "I usually sit in the middle somewhere, but it doesn't matter."

I grab her wrist and steer her toward three empty chairs at the end of a row that's closer to the back. Kristin trails behind us, planting herself on the end with me in the middle and Brynne on the other side of me.

I nudge Brynne. "Relax. No one here bites."

She throws me a dirty look.

Yeah, she'll be fine.

I wish I could take the credit for her being here tonight, but honestly, Brynne invited herself. Well, not *exactly*. But the conversation about my church came up again one night when we were hanging out, and she straight out asked if she could come with me to our next youth night. And . . . well, here we are.

I'm nervous about what she'll think about my church and youth group, but I'm still glad she came.

Anthony opens with prayer and goes over the announcements for a fundraiser the youth are putting on for a mission trip coming up in three months. His eyes meet mine before slipping over to Brynne. He gives her a welcoming nod. "It's good to have Alli's friend here with us tonight."

I didn't get a chance to catch him before class to introduce him to Brynne. I feel bad that he can't welcome her by name.

Anthony then turns the service over to Brother McGuire,

who speaks to us for the next thirty minutes about being part of the family of God.

It's exactly what I wanted Brynne to hear—not that anyone asked my opinion or anything. It's just that, when you bring a visitor to church and it might be the only chance you'll get them there, you want the message to hit home.

I think it does because when I sneak a side glance over at Brynne, she's really locked in on Brother McGuire and seems to be soaking it all in.

I work on trying to relax since my back is getting stiff and starting to ache from tension. I haven't sat this still since our high school principal had to stand in as a substitute in my algebra class last semester. If you met my principal, you'd get what I mean. I sink back against the seat and give the message my full attention.

When Brother McGuire asks for a call to pray, several teens make their way out of their seats and gather around the front. A few girls huddle close to pray together, and two of the young men kneel by the chairs at the front. Everyone prays in their own way, some remaining in their seats to pray. After a moment, Kristin slips into the center aisle and makes her way to the front as well.

There are only four or five of us left that aren't praying and it feels awkward. I know the thing I *should* do is ask Brynne if she'd like to pray. But I don't know if that's something she's ever really done before. Maybe she has no idea how to start. Maybe she's waiting for me to lead the way or make the first move.

I'm about to bow my head to pray where we are—you

know, to set an example for Brynne—when she leans toward me and whispers, "Um, do we go up there to pray?" She points toward the front where many of the others have gathered.

Okay . . . I wasn't expecting that.

I nod, since I don't know what else to do. I feel dumb that she had to mention it first. I mean, we *are* on my turf at this point. I should've taken the lead on this. "Sure, let's go."

Once we're standing up front together, I'm relieved to see Kristin making her way over to us. There was a time in the past when her boldness with her faith annoyed me, but I'm glad she's taking the initiative right now. She comes in close to Brynne and asks, "Is there anything you want us to pray with you about?"

Brynne hesitates for a moment, then answers, "Yeah, um, can we pray for my grandpa? He's not doing too good right now."

Kristin comes around and reaches for my hand, and I latch on to Brynne's. For the next few minutes, the only thing I hear is our voices quietly blending together in prayer for Brynne's grandpa.

In my heart, her grandpa isn't the only one I am praying for. I'm asking for forgiveness for myself for how I've shut God out lately. I'm also praying for God to work on Brynne and help her know him in a deeper way, for Tessa and all that she's facing, and for her mom, dad, and her brother, Aaron.

I almost find myself praying for Kim, Shanice, and . . . Chad.

But I can't. I just *can't.*

"YOU NEED to have a talk with Tessa."

Brynne throws her backpack on the bench between us and plops down.

I freeze in the middle of tearing the burnt edge off my cheese quesadilla. Our school lunch bar doesn't have too bad of a selection, but they fall short in the Mexican food department.

I stare at Brynne over the top of a piece of torn tortilla. "What do you mean?"

"I heard Shanice talking to another girl—she was sitting behind me in study hall—about a big party going down tonight at Chad's house."

I shrug and take a bite of my food, instantly disconnected. "So what? There are always parties going down at Chad's." I still get defensive at the mention of his name. "Tessa goes to them all the time. Why is this party such a big deal?"

"Because, Miss Act-Like-I'm-Not-Interested," Brynne tilts her cup of iced tea my way and jabs the end of her straw into the air for emphasis, "Shanice was saying something about a bunch of college kids planning to be there and about how there's going to be some 'heavy stuff' going down. They were carrying on about Chad's cousin and some other guys' names I've never heard of, not that I would know who they are anyway." She takes a sip of her tea, "It sounds like some bad stuff, Alli."

"Okay . . . point taken," I say, "But I still don't get why this has anything to do with me. What Tessa does is her business."

I try to toss the rest of the quesadilla into a nearby trash bin and miss. I'll pick it up in a minute. "Why don't *you* talk to Tessa if you're so worried about her?"

My words come out harsher than I'd planned, so I give her sad eyes to soften the blow. "Besides, it's not like I can just walk up to Tessa these days and tell her I'm concerned about her choices. She wouldn't give me the time of day, and honestly, she's not my problem. We aren't even friends anymore, so I don't owe her any loyalty."

Brynne just stares at me.

I throw my hands up and shrug. "She's a big girl, Brynne. She'll figure it out sooner or later."

Brynne looks disappointed in me but she understands that Tessa and I are no longer friends. She probably just figures I'm the only hope Tessa has at this point. Frankly, I'm impressed Brynne even cares about what happens to Tessa either.

As much as I try to convince myself that I've completely written Tessa off, Brynne's warning about her hits home. I hide my concern behind my attitude though because it just feels safer to keep the mask on for Brynne.

I'm curious why it's even on Brynne's radar that Tessa's going to a party where shady things might be going down. Brynne and Tessa haven't spoken in months, and they were never really *friends* in the first place. Plus, if Brynne knew the shocking choice Tessa made not long ago, Tessa going to this party would be no worse than if she'd made a toddler cry by popping their balloon. Then again, maybe that choice wouldn't shock Brynne as much as it did me.

"Don't you care, Alli?" Brynne asks. "This isn't just going to be some off-the-charts high school party. She's messing with the big boys now."

Since Brynne's been coming to church recently, I want to be careful not to damage her newfound faith in God. It's not that Brynne doesn't expect me to have hurt feelings over Tessa, but she's probably having a hard time understanding why I'm not more compassionate toward her. And to be honest, justified or not, I'm having a hard time understanding it myself.

"Listen, Brynne," I say, "I know Tessa's getting involved in stuff way over her head, but she's going into it with eyes wide open. She knows what she's doing. And if she doesn't, maybe it's time for her to learn."

I'm trying to play tough, but I can feel old wounds festering that I'd prefer weren't disturbed. I don't want my response to sound too personal, but it *is* personal, whether I want to acknowledge it or not. I can't help it either, and that frustrates me.

I push my wounded pride's intrusive head back down where it came from. "Sorry, Brynne. I don't mean to sound heartless, but it's not my problem what happens to Tessa anymore."

I LIED.

As much as I *want* to not care about what happens to Tessa and to leave her at the mercy of the choices she made—including turning her back on her best friend—my heart holds on to that one fragile thread of what we once shared.

I don't agree with my heart, and I don't appreciate its meddling around with my logic, but my heart tends to do its own thing with or without my approval.

I can't get Chad's party out of my mind. I tell myself it's just morbid curiosity that Brynne's stirred in me, but, well . . . that's what I mean about my heart just shoving its way into the middle of everything, like a persistent puppy nipping at my ankle. My heart wins. I'm going to check this party out and check on Tessa.

Even at the risk of seeing Chad.

I tell myself I'll just make sure no one is burning the house down or setting off illegal fireworks—whatever I imagine might happen at a wild party. I reason that I'll be in and out and back home safe and sound in no time.

The back door makes a soft *click* as I ease it closed. My lungs scream for air, but I ignore them until I'm safely off the back porch and moving across the grass, avoiding the floodlight that's mounted to the back corner of the house.

When I finally make it through the back fence, I suck in a gallon of air and watch for any movement from the house.

Relieved to see that no alarms have been raised, I move toward a line of trees that will provide cover for me until I can make it to the street.

I'm almost there when my toe catches the edge of a broken bottle and sends it careening straight toward a trash can. The impact against the empty metal container sets off an impromptu chorus of dog reactions ranging from bellowing altos to screeching sopranos, and I'm forced to freeze in place again until the serenade's over.

I think of the night Tessa and I snuck out to spy on Chad's party. That night, we were hiding in the bushes like nerdy middle schoolers who didn't get the invite, but it was still a thrill.

When I finally went to a real party *with* Chad, it wasn't as exciting as I imagined it would be. I was the outsider staring wide-eyed at sights that were foreign to me, peering over my shoulder like a lamb in a lion's den, and failing miserably at trying to mimic everyone's body language and party-speak. I was a walking billboard that read, "Newbie in the House."

I hated every minute of it.

It made me feel exactly like the thing I despise feeling the most: *different.*

But here I am in the bushes again, trying to sneak a peek at a party from the outside. Only this time, I'm alone and twice as freaked out.

At least there's no manic dog barking in the yard next door this time.

I feel awful about sneaking out again, knowing that I'm betraying my parents' trust and that I would be totally busted if they found out. But my intentions are honorable. Not that my parents would agree or care about my "honorable intentions," but I can't deny that, despite all that's come between us, I really do care about what happens to Tessa.

I'm probably overthinking this. This party might turn out to be nothing but wasted time in the bushes for me and I'll see nothing more than a bunch of drunk teenagers hanging out.

But what if major stuff *does* go down at this party tonight? Could I even do anything about it? Maybe I'd be helping Tessa avoid a potentially serious situation if I call the police and left an anonymous tip. Of course, then I'd need proof, and they'd wonder what I was doing here in the first place.

Never mind. Too risky. Better to hold off on that idea.

I move out from behind the prickly bush—probably the same one Tessa and I got tangled in the night we were spying— and move closer to the fence. People move inside, but I can't make out faces or details.

Naturally, I can't hear anything besides the head-pounding music blasting out through the open windows and sliding doors at the back of the house. I'm sure the neighbors for miles around appreciate the boisterous clamor, especially at eleven o'clock at night.

I jump back into the shadows when a group of teenagers stumble out onto the back porch, laughing and shoving each other as they make their way to a couple of swinging benches facing the swimming pool. One tall, red-headed guy swerves and almost falls into the pool, prompting a round of hoots and catcalls from his friends. I scan their faces and recognize several of them from school.

I rub my arms and wonder why I didn't think to bring a jacket. There's a lot I didn't think about before slipping away to snoop on this party. What did I think I was going to see from the back fence? Like some shifty college guys would come to a party to make connections and who-knows-what-else by just wandering around in the backyard? Of course not. They'd be in the thick of things inside, chumming it up with the partygoers.

I need to get closer. But how?

I shiver in the dark shadows like a nervous cat, trying to think of a plan through the sensory overload from the rowdy group by the pool and the head-pounding music knocking against my eardrums.

I'm about to call it a night and forget the whole thing when I see Shanice walk past the kitchen window. Just the sight of her makes my stomach knot with anger and . . . *hatred* would be too strong of a word, but the sight of her makes me want to stab my fingers in someone's eyes.

I throw my head back and stare up at the stars, hoping one of them will beam a great idea down to me.

Nothing.

I'm reduced to doing something dumb and desperate, which is exactly how I usually get myself in more trouble. But I don't stop to think; I just start walking.

It isn't until I reach the front porch that I look down at myself and notice the plain denim skirt and striped T-shirt I'd worn to school. It's not that I think there's a dress code to get in or anything, but I'm sure most people would've at least changed their shirt if they had a spaghetti stain on the front like I do.

Oh well.

I don't bother knocking because, one, not one soul would hear me over the racket, and two, no one knocks at these kinds of parties, as I learned after going with Chad to one. These are the kinds of parties where the homeless could find a few hours to hang out in a warm place and maybe grab a handful chips, without ever being noticed. In fact, they could probably catch some sleep in a corner somewhere, and no one would be the wiser.

The music is ten times louder before I even peel back the screen door. Three girls block the doorway, and I have to duck under one girl's elbow before I'm fully in.

I'm surprised and sort of proud of myself for making it this far. I can feel the stares, and some guy asks me if I'm lost and want some company.

I ignore it all while I look for some sign of Tessa.

A burly guy with a long black goatee (which *no one* has in my high school) sits on the floor, leaning against the wall near the entrance to the dining room. His arms are wrapped around a girl I know from school who sits on his lap, messing with her phone and giggling at whatever he's saying in her ear. Neither of them notice me until I have to step over them and end up tripping, jamming my shoulder into a huge, wooden bookcase.

I glare down at them, but they just give me a dirty look before the girl says, "Watch where you're going." I take one look at the burly dude's angry scowl and keep walking, watching closely for any more legs sprawled in my path.

"Alli?"

I don't see her until the two guys with her turn to look, leaving a gap between them.

I guess I found Tessa. Or, should I say, she found *me*.

Tessa's dressed in a miniskirt with a black sweater cardigan that hangs to her hips and slides off one bare shoulder. Her face is flushed, and her makeup is so overdone that she looks plastic. Even the stiff way she holds herself reminds me of a department store mannequin. I wonder how long it's been since I've really paid attention to how she's changed.

The two guys with her—one short with dark skin and fierce eyes, the other tall with long, black hair plastered to his forehead with a layer of either sweat or hair grease—post themselves on each side of her like two rottweilers guarding a favorite steak bone.

I've never seen either one of these guys before. Something feels way off, and my blood turns icy under my skin. I fix my eyes on Tessa but can't shake the chills that run laps up and down my spine.

"Tessa, um, hey—"

"What are you doing here, Alli?"

Tessa's eyes flash dark for a second like she's irritated I'm here, but then they soften as if she suddenly realizes she's glad to see me.

She looks past me as if to see who I came with. Seeing no one, she locks her eyes back on me. "Why are you here?" she repeats, irritation winning over. "You should be home."

There's a hint of panic and something else in her eyes but, before I can interpret it, her attention breaks away to the dark-skinned dude with freakish eyes.

I'm having a hard time hearing Tessa with all the noise, and I feel a sudden need to be closer to her, so I step forward. My eyes dart between the two guys.

An urgency I can't identify comes over me. I say the first thing that comes to mind. "Uh, Aaron called me looking for you." The lie slides easily off my tongue.

Tessa looks back at me. I study her face closely, but my internal radar is on hyper-alert. At this point, I can almost hear my heart pounding above the music.

"My *brother*, Aaron?" Tessa's face is a mask of doubt. I need to think fast to convince her.

"Yeah . . . He, uh, said you weren't answering your phone."

Her brows pull together, and I know she's wavering. Turning her head, Tessa does a slow survey of the room. I gather she's left her phone somewhere, which isn't like her. She's never without her phone.

I hope she doesn't go looking for it, because one push of a button will reveal that she has no missed calls, at least not from her brother.

I look over at the shorter, dark guy and notice that he's glaring at me. The taller one turns to Tessa, partially blocking my view, and says something to her.

I take another step forward. "Tessa, can I talk to you outside for a minute?" When her attention's back on me, I jerk my head toward the front door, but she's too distracted to notice.

Mr. Dark-and-Mysterious grunts and shakes his head. He stares right at me but addresses Tessa. "Oh, how sweet. Little brother's checking up on you. You gotta be home by curfew, sweetheart?" Even with all the noise around us, I don't miss the sarcasm dripping in his voice.

Tessa punches him on the arm with a glare. "Shut up, Drew." She starts to push past him but ends up stumbling and almost loses her balance.

Drew—which is a much more charming name than this guy deserves—catches her by the arm and steadies her. "Whoa, watch yourself, hon."

When Tessa looks back at me, she seems disoriented and confused. I can't tell if she's had too much to drink, or if she's sick, or . . . something worse than both.

I move closer. "Are you okay, Tessa?"

She tugs her arm from Drew and shakes her head. "I'm fine, Alli. I'll call Aaron later."

I don't take my eyes off her. "Are you sure? Because, um . . . Aaron sounded like he really needed to talk to you." I try to sound gruff and strong, but my nerves are on edge. I ignore the fear and pin my attention on my best friend.

"Do you know these guys, Tessa?" I plead with her with my eyes, and my heart is doing that "don't think, just do something" thing again.

"Who are you? Her *mother*? She told you to leave her alone," the greasy-haired guy says.

"She never asked me to leave her alone," I retort, my fear shoved to the back burner now.

"Alli, seriously, everything's fine," Tessa says. "You need to go." She takes a step back from Drew, who watches her every move. Her color looks better, but she still doesn't look herself.

"I'm just hanging out, alright?" she says. "Besides, it's none of your business if I know these guys or not."

How many times have I heard "it's none of your business" from Tessa now? I'm starting to lose count.

I try to search Tessa's eyes in case she might be trying to send me a silent message, but she's already dismissed me and looks around the perimeter of the room, probably looking for her phone again.

Drew turns my way and continues to stare at me, his eyes black, ominous, glassy, and shifty. *Is he high on something?* I wonder.

I stare back, taking in all the details of his dark face. Though I try to read his expression, I can't figure out why this guy makes me feel like I'm standing too close to a burning flame and need to back away or be scorched.

I shudder, my eyes flicking to Tessa, who's somehow retrieved her phone and is scrolling through it. She's seconds away from finding out that there were no calls from her brother. I just hope it makes her wonder what I'm really doing here, why I would go out of my way to show up at this party— alone—and lie to her.

But I'm starting to lose that hope.

I look back at the two guys pinning Tessa in. The tall, nameless guy is talking to some girl behind him. Focusing back on Drew, I see one corner of his mouth lift, and he gives me a slow wink. Then, he turns and nudges himself against Tessa, completely cutting off my view.

I'm done.

I don't know why I wasted my time and risked getting in trouble for this—for Tessa. The only redeeming comfort I have is that I acted on Brynne's warning about Tessa and this party and tried to give Tessa a way out. Now, I have to focus on taking care of myself and figure out how I'm going to sneak back into my house.

Plus, I know I smell like an ashtray just from being in this house, and the haze of smoke drifting around me is making my eyes water. A raging headache is coming on from the loud music pulsating against my skull, and I'll probably hear ringing in my ears for days after this.

Before I make it to the front door though, Shanice appears in front of me, blocking my escape.

"What are *you* doing here?" she asks.

I'm sick to death of being asked this question by everyone.

"Chad has a real girlfriend now, church girl." Her laugh is screechy and grinds like nails on a chalkboard with the headache I've got coming on.

With the way I'm feeling right now, I could easily start throwing punches and tearing Shanice's hair out in fistfuls.

"Move, Shanice," I say. "I'm not dealing with you right now."

I start to brush past her, but she doesn't budge, and I can't quite fit in the empty space between her and the doorway. "I said *move*, Shanice."

I'm so frustrated and angry at this point, I don't know what I'll do. Apparently, Shanice gets the same vibe because she scoots over a whole three inches, which is all I need. I force past her this time, rubbing a few skin cells off her arm as I go.

"It's too bad Chad didn't lead you on a little longer. We were all enjoying the show," she sneers.

I spin around and thrust my face just inches from hers. Her breath stinks like booze, but I'm ready for a fight and have no intention of letting her comment slide. But instead of throwing myself at Shanice, my eyes are drawn toward a long, black material swooping out the back sliding door followed closely by the two hounds who've been glued to Tessa since I arrived.

Then, a couple people move into my line of vision. I lose sight of Tessa for a second before they move on, and she comes into my line of sight again. I notice her stumble over a planter on the back porch before the glass door slides closed and she's lost to me.

I spot her cell phone on the dining room table before my view is blocked again.

She must've set it down after she saw there wasn't anything from Aaron. Why wouldn't she just keep it on her?

A thousand questions fill my head before I reign them in and refocus.

Something's wrong.

"Where are they going?" I ask, pointing to the sliding door and glaring up at Shanice, who stares at me like I've lost my mind. "Is there a gate in the backyard?"

Shanice turns her head to see what I'm talking about, and I brush past her. I sprint out the front door and down the front steps.

After pausing for a second to get my bearings, I break into a jog toward the side of the house where I see an old, black sports car—I don't know enough about cars to identify the model—with its lights on and someone sitting in the driver's seat.

It's not out of the ordinary, but when I see Tessa and Drew slide into the backseat and the tall guy hop up in front with the driver, I get the sick sensation that this whole scene is anything *but* ordinary.

Even if Tessa knows these guys, I can't think of any acceptable reason she would be getting in the car with three guys, none of whom I've seen before tonight, and leave the party. Besides, I don't like the way she looked: like she wasn't herself and kind of dazed. Or the way she seemed so clumsy and out of it.

I step under the streetlight and start waving my hands, but the driver peels out and makes a U-turn in the middle of the street, racing down the road the opposite way.

My heart bangs in my chest, and I realize I'm breathing like I've run a marathon, even though I'm standing still.

I'm a statue of shock as I try to process what I just saw. The panic wells up in me, and I know I need to do something, but I have no clue what that *something* is.

Racing back to the front porch, I consider going back to the party to make a scene and get someone to help me but, the problem is, I doubt anyone *would* help me.

Instead, they'd probably just think that I'm a nutcase or that I'd been drinking and don't know what I'm talking about. Plus, there's still that part of me that hates calling attention to myself—even if it's for a good cause.

I can see why they would think I'm weird too. Lots of

people go off with each other at parties, sometimes just to hop over to another party somewhere else. What would I even say? Would I walk into the middle of the party and yell out, "Hey, I just saw Tessa get in the car with three guys I don't know?"

Yeah, right, after the Chad ordeal and whatever else Shanice and Kim have told everyone about me, I already know the response I'd get. I'd be the laughingstock of the party and would just be giving them another free show. Another round of juicy gossip to spread.

I can't face that again.

So instead of making a scene, I slip back into the party—keeping one eye out for Shanice and another out for Chad—and duck under arms and around bodies as I work my way to Tessa's cell phone, which is still sitting on the dining room table.

A quick glance around tells me that no one's noticed it sitting there, so I slide it into my pocket and make a beeline back to the front door.

Outside, I lower myself to the top porch step and fish out my own cell phone. I'm still breathing heavy, and the storm brewing in my chest pushes upward into my throat until it finally bursts forth with a torrent of tears.

This doesn't feel like it's going to end well for anyone, but I know it's the right thing to do, because the only person I hope it *does* end well for is Tessa.

God, be with Tessa right now. I pray. *Don't let her do something stupid.* Though according to what I've seen tonight, she already has.

On the third ring, my dad picks up.

"Dad? It's Alli."

"What? *Who?* Alli?"

His voice is groggy and muffled. It takes a second for him to register that I'm calling his cell phone when my bedroom's just down the hall. There's a soft grunt, and I know he's making his way to my room, thinking I'm there.

I decide to save him the shock.

"Dad, just listen. Please don't wake Mom up yet. I need to tell you something first."

It takes me several tries to get the whole story out while my dad listens quietly.

He's always like that: listens first, reacts second.

"Ok, honey. Don't leave. I'm on my way," he says.

After we hang up, I hit the next contact in my phone.

Chapter Thirty-One

I don't want Mom to hear it from Dad. She would've ended up calling me anyway if she had.

I'm crying so hard I can't even get the words out.

"Alli? Why are you calling me on the phone instead of just walking—"

"I'm not at home, Mom."

"What are you talking about? Where are you?"

I'm forced to cup my hand over the phone so she can hear me over the music. I have no problem hearing *her* since she's in high-decibel panic mode.

"Mom, just listen. I snuck out—I'll explain later—but I came to a party to check on Tessa, and . . ." I stop, knowing I'm probably not making sense, and try to start over. ". . . what I'm trying to say is —"

"A *party*? What are you doing at a . . . *what* party? You aren't in your room? Alli, *what is going on*?"

There's a shuffling sound and a low groan. I imagine my

mom clawing her way out of the bedsheets and reaching in the dark for her slippers next to the bed. I hear the tremble in her voice even though she's making a brave attempt to be angry.

I know I'm scaring her, but I can't do anything about that.

"Tony?" I can tell she's in their bathroom, calling for Dad, thinking he might be there.

I know Dad's already on his way. I told him I was calling Mom to let her know. He agreed since he knew that, if he told Mom, she would weigh him down with questions and probably insist on coming, wasting precious time.

"Dad's not home. He's coming to pick me up."

"Alli! My goodness. First off, are you okay? What do you mean your dad's coming?"

There's a dull sound of a drawer opening, and I know she's digging around for something to change into.

"Are you sure you're safe?" she asks, sounding out of breath.

"I'm okay, Mom. Honest. Just listen. It's Tessa. She . . . I saw her leave with some guys. Some older guys I've never seen before. Guys at the party—"

"*Leave*? What do you mean by *leave*? Alli, honey, tell me where you are. And what do you mean you've never seen these guys—"

"Mom, wait."

I know all she wants is to be assured that I'm okay—that I'm safe—before she's willing to hear about Tessa.

"I promise, Mom. I'm okay. I'm sitting outside of a guy's house from school. It's where the party was—*is*—at. Everyone's inside. They don't even know I'm out here."

I'm still gulping in air, trying to calm myself, but I *am* starting to feel a little more in control.

"I'll explain more later. Like I said, Dad's on his way to get me."

"How did I not hear him leave?" She says. "What in the world? Why did you call your dad and not me? He's picking you up right now?"

"Yes, Dad's coming. I'll explain when I get home. I promise."

Why *did* I call my mom anyway? All she's going to do is worry until I get home.

I guess I just needed to hear her voice. Even at seventeen, a girl still needs her mom. Especially since I can't bear to sit here alone with my fear and guilt, completely stressing over Tessa with no one to talk me down. Then again, I'm not sure why I would call my mom if I need someone to talk me down since she's freaking out as much as I am and doesn't even know the whole story yet. Still, I feel calmer just hearing her voice.

"Alright, hon. How long ago did you talk to your dad? He's on his way *right now*?" A rhythmic tingling sound tells me she's pushing through hangers in her closet.

"Mom. You don't need to get dressed. Just stay home with Avery. Dad's almost here." I'm really hoping that I'm right.

A frustrated sigh comes from the other side of the line, but I think she's finally put the brakes on.

"How soon?" she asks.

Snot runs down my lip, and I wipe it on my shirt sleeve. Who cares at this point? Vanity's not high on my priority list right now.

I look down at Tessa's phone sitting next to me on the step. The flood comes again.

"Um," I hiccup through a sob, "I just talked to him a few minutes ago. He said he was about—"

A flash of headlights blares in my face, blinding me. I scoop everything from the step and make my way down the steps, praying it's my dad.

"Hang on, Mom, this might be him."

When the lights spin into a nearby driveway, I back up into the shadows next to the porch steps. The music thumps from every cavity of the house, and there are spurts of laughter and carrying on, but the excitement I felt an hour ago drains out until I feel nothing but an avalanche of regret crashing down on me. A cool breeze brushes my face, and the tears dry to a crust in my eyes. I guessed I'm cried out for now, but I know I'm far from done for the night.

"Alli? Is it your dad?"

"Sorry. No, it was a neighbor. Mom, I know I have some explaining to do and all, but could you . . . you know, pray for Tessa? I don't know if she's in trouble or anything; it's just that I don't feel good about her right now."

"Tell me what's going on, Alli," Mom says. "You're scaring me. Do we need to call the police? I'm going to call Debbie and Paul after I get off the phone with you, but I'm not hanging up until I know Dad's there."

Now I feel sick. Of course, I know someone should call Tessa's parents, but the idea of pulling other people into this —*the police?*—makes it so much more serious. I mean, what if Tessa's just fine and we're making a way bigger deal of this than it needs to be? If Tessa shows up safe at home later, I'm going to look like a total idiot drama queen. She'd never speak to me again.

"I don't know, Mom!" *Gosh, I just don't know.* "I don't know what's going on or if you need to call the police. Yeah, I think you should call her parents for sure. Well . . ."

Mom doesn't know about Tessa's parents and the divorce yet, I realize. And Tessa's mom already looked like a vase about to shatter into a million pieces the last time I saw her.

"You better call her dad. He handles things better than Mrs. Williams, and he'll know what to do."

I'll have to tell her the rest of the story later. *It looks like I'm going to be doing a lot of talking later, like it or not.*

I'm almost positive Tessa's *not* okay. Sure, she might show up later, but I bet she won't be doing all that great after how out of it she looked when I last saw her. She doesn't even have her cell phone. And I didn't look to see if her purse was around, so that might mean she doesn't have her wallet or an ID either. If she's out of it all night, how will those guys, or whoever she catches a ride from, even know where to drop her off?

I don't have it in me to go back into the house to check for her purse. I'll let the adults take it from here.

Then, the thought occurs to me that the guys she was with might just bring her back here to the party. That they'll get tired or bored and decide to call it a night.

I'm about to suggest to my mom that Dad and I should stay here, but I cringe imagining Dad seeing where I chanced sneaking out and snooping around and, worse yet, imagining that he might go check out what's happening and who's at this party. I'm sure the minute he turns down the street, gets close to the house, and hears the raging party dominating the whole neighborhood, he'll already be well aware of what I got myself into.

Which means that the right thing to do is still to call Tessa's parents—at least her dad to start with—and let them know what's going on and give them the address to where the party is. The adults can ask around and find out who the guys were and where they might have gone with Tessa.

Another set of headlights floods the street up ahead, and Dad's red truck comes into view.

"Dad's here," I tell my mom. "Listen, Mom. Dad can call Tessa's parents when I get in the car with him. They're going to ask questions you won't know the answers to, and I can give them the address to the house we were at tonight."

She agrees and waits until I confirm that Dad has pulled up to the house before she hangs up with an "I love you" and "I'm praying."

What she doesn't say but I *know* is coming is: "And you have some serious explaining to do."

The bile rises in my throat as I open the truck door. As much as I know he loves me, I don't want to face my dad, and I absolutely do *not* want to make that call to Tessa's father.

Chapter Thirty-Two

It's the fifth time—*maybe the sixth?*—that I've checked my phone. I've lost count of how many times I've picked it up and looked at the screen, its bright glow cutting into my aching eyes like sharp glass, the illumination from the screen the only light in the room.

2:47

In a few hours, the sun will be up, and I'll probably still be awake to greet it. Even though I'm exhausted, there's no way I can sleep after the night I've had and without knowing where Tessa is and what's happening with her.

The police and Tessa's parents left around one-thirty after interviewing the people at Chad's party—the ones that were still there, anyway—and coming here to interview me and collect Tessa's phone. They told us they also found her wallet at Chad's house.

The question the police hit me with that really haunts me

the most is: "What kind of mental and physical state was Tessa in when you last saw her?"

That was the hardest question for me to answer. I broke out crying all over again.

I could feel everyone's eyes boring into me while I tried to answer as truthfully as possible. I knew my words were going to hurt Tessa's parents the most.

"Tessa seemed, well . . . out of it. She acted like she wasn't all there, you know?"

The female police officer stared at me with narrow eyes like she knew I had more to say but was holding back.

I took a breath and tried again. "I know Tessa pretty well, and I think she was high or drunk . . ." I knew my parents were probably wondering how I could make a judgment call on something I'm not supposed to know much about. And to be honest, I *don't* know much about it. But it doesn't take a rocket scientist to know when someone's under the influence of something stronger than just an energy drink. "Or something like that," I finished lamely.

I couldn't even look at Tessa's parents when I described how she was hanging with those two guys I'd never seen before who didn't go to our school and who I was pretty sure were older than high schoolers.

I told the police how Brynne had even warned me that she'd overheard that some bad things were supposed to go down at the party and that I should warn Tessa. So naturally, Brynne's next on their list to talk to, making me feel even worse.

"That's why I snuck out," I offered to my parents, trying to make them understand my motive.

Dad's face was grave. "You should've come to us first."

"I know, Dad. I'm so sorry."

I gave the police the best description I could of the two guys, giving details about the dark, creepy guy and how he challenged me when I tried to pull Tessa's attention away. I didn't have much on the taller guy, but I gave all the details I had. I cringed just describing them to the police, so I can't imagine what horrors were going through Tessa's parents' minds.

I described the car Tessa and the guys got into the best I could, but I couldn't describe the driver at all since it was so dark. Plus, I was too busy feeling scared and shell-shocked at the time for my brain to catalog any of the important details that I had no clue I'd need later.

The police also asked Tessa's parents several questions, including the possibility of Tessa being a runaway. They told the police they didn't think that was the case. Before they left, the police assured us that they would enter Tessa's name into a database of missing minors and would continue their investigation. Other than that, unfortunately, all any of us could do was wait.

And now, here I am, staring at the light seeping through the bottom of my bedroom door, knowing my parents are still awake too, out in the living room praying—something I should've been doing way before this long night started, which leaves me feeling like a complete failure. In fact, some serious praying may have helped keep Tessa out of danger too. Who knows? It couldn't have hurt the situation.

Like I knew they would, the tears flood over again. Most are for Tessa, some are for myself, and some are for Tessa's parents, who I know are in shock and are facing unimaginable fear right now. There's no doubt in my mind they're checking their phone more often than I am right now and that sleep probably won't come for them tonight either.

I knew I shouldn't have left her last night. I mean, I know I was wrong to be there in the first place, and it doesn't matter that Tessa no longer thinks of me as *her* best friend; she's still mine.

Tessa had no idea what she was doing. I'm clueless about how much she drank or, God forbid, whatever else she may have inhaled or swallowed. I should've been watching out for her. I should've been her eyes and ears and dragged her out of there while I still could.

She probably wouldn't have listened to me anyway, but I didn't even *try*.

At least my conscience would've felt better if I'd at least tried to do *something*.

I shove my face in my pillow and sob until my chest feels like it's caving in. And I pray, wishing I'd been doing that all along. Maybe I could've even saved myself from falling for Chad and getting hurt if I'd been praying and keeping my head in the game instead of blindly prancing after him.

Well, better late than never, right? I'm just hoping it isn't too late to make a difference for my best friend.

"Where are you, Tessa?" I whisper into the dark room. "I'm worried about you."

~

THE COFFEE SHOP's filling up with the evening crowd, and I can tell Anthony's getting antsy about offering our table to other patrons since we've had this one for over an hour now. That's Anthony for you—always the considerate one.

I take a sip of my iced white chocolate mocha and sit back in my chair, in no hurry to leave. I've enjoyed our time together tonight. Looking around at the cozy little reading corner and the huge, oak display shelf of new releases, I wonder why I don't come here more often. Books are my love language (I have an impressive collection of my own in my room), and just being around them makes me feel calm and happy.

"Alli, can I grab one of your sticky notes?" Brynne taps her pen against the notepad in front of me, interrupting my calm, happy moment.

"Oh, yeah, sure."

I push the notepad closer to her and watch as she jots something down, peels the note off the pad, and smooths it onto a page in her Bible before snapping it closed.

She pushes the Bible into her purse and hands me the notepad. "Thanks."

Anthony's already standing, gathering up the napkins and wiping crumbs off the table from Brynne's peanut butter cookie.

I still have my notebook and stuff spread out on the table. I'm bummed about leaving already but know we can't hog the table all night.

Brynne, Anthony, and I have been meeting here on

Wednesday nights over the past couple of weeks for Bible study. Brynne's been coming to youth nights for a while now and plans to come this Sunday for her first regular service. Anthony asked her one night after youth class if she would be interested in a Bible study and asked that I join them. I wasn't sure about it at first, but I'm glad I did.

Brynne's been my rock since the night Tessa went missing. She even forgave me for spilling the beans that it was her who warned me about the party that night and has been the first to volunteer to pass out flyers and post signs with Tessa's photo and information on them.

I started sharing more of my faith with Brynne and reading the Bible with her, and although I thought I was helping save *her*, she was really saving *me*. Talking and sharing my faith with Brynne helped to keep me focused on something positive instead of being obsessed with worry over Tessa.

I hope I can find the words someday to tell her how much her friendship has meant to me over these past months.

"I gotta head out," Anthony says, giving us the peace sign as he leaves.

"Bye, Anthony. See you on Sunday." Brynne gives a little wave.

"See you, Anthony." I nod and start organizing my stuff to get ready to leave.

Brynne has her things all packed up and scrolls through her phone, waiting for me. She's my ride tonight, so I hope she'll go for walking around for a few minutes before we leave. I'm anxious to browse over the mystery book selection for something new to read.

Before I even open my mouth to ask, a shadow falls across our table, and a voice behind me says, "Oh, wow, is that a Bible?"

I don't even have to look to know that the annoying voice belongs to Shanice.

Brynne glances up from her phone, and I catch the defiant look on her face. I know she isn't in the mood for dealing with Shanice any more than I am.

I'm about to turn around and throw a snarky reply at Shanice, but a spark of reasoning stops me in my tracks. Brynne's here for a Bible study tonight, and I've been trying to be an example to her and show her God's love. If I lay into Shanice right now, I'll be undoing everything I've been trying to live up to for Brynne.

It's like swallowing bile lodged in my throat, but I force myself to look up at Shanice and smile.

"Hey, Shanice."

I look down at my Bible with its dusty pink cover and rose-colored tabs that I'd carefully added myself. "Yeah, it's mine," I say. "What's up?" As if I need to ask, when I know exactly what's *always* up with Shanice: trouble.

I chance a quick peek around for Kim, who's usually not far behind, but see no sign of her.

Shanice toys with the leather tassels on her belt as she looks down at me, ignoring Brynne, who wears a scowl but doesn't say a word.

Brynne's simmering vibes fill the space between us.

"Oh, well isn't that *adorable*?" Shanice says. "Are you guys"

—she drops the belt tassel and waggles a finger between Brynne and me—"like, reading the Bible together?"

I know she's mocking us, but I don't play into it. It's time for me to respond like a big girl, like it or not. To be the *good old Alli* I seem to always be running from.

Be different, I think, and cringe.

I turn around in my chair so I'm fully facing Shanice, and rest one arm on the back of my chair, trying to appear casual and send a message that her patronizing attitude isn't ruffling me, when in fact, it *is* ruffling me.

"Yeah, actually, we were."

I glance at Brynne for confirmation, but she's still locked on Shanice and doesn't notice. I turn back to Shanice.

"Would you like to join us?"

I'd rather walk on hot lava than have Shanice join us, but I throw it out there anyway.

Her condescending sneer provides the answer. "How generous, Alli, but I'm not really *into* religion. That's *your* thing." Her finger waggles again. "Not mine." She looks over at Brynne, who continues to glare at her.

I can tell by the smirk forming on Shanice's face that she's about to start directing her poison darts at Brynne, and I know the outcome will go downhill from there. So, I jerk my tote from the floor, slide my books from the table down into it, and stand.

"Well, that's too bad, Shanice," I say. "We really need to go anyway." I look to Brynne, who stands and reaches for her bag, not nearly in as much of a hurry as I am.

Shanice has no choice but to move when my chair jabs against her tennis shoe, which was blocking the chair leg.

Without waiting for Brynne or for any more comments from Shanice, I make my way to the exit, hoping Brynne follows behind me.

I guess I'm going to have to browse for mystery books another night.

Chapter Thirty-Three

THE CALL FINALLY COMES TONIGHT.

The call that everyone's been holding their breath and losing sleep waiting for, praying for, and agonizing over.

I'm chopping potatoes for dinner at the kitchen counter when I hear Dad's cell phone ring in the office. Then, I hear him say, "Paul? *What*? There's news about Tessa?"

I freeze with the knife poised over an uncut potato, straining to listen, wavering between running to the office or passing out cold on the kitchen floor.

I know something—either horrible or miraculous—is up right away when my mom starts crying. The knife drops onto the cutting board as I back away from the counter. My body breaks out in a cold sweat and I can't move. Time stands still.

Then, I hear my mom saying, "Thank you, Jesus," over and over.

Somehow, I find my legs and race to the office, parking myself in front of my dad while he finishes his conversation with Mr. Williams. My hand searches for Mom's, and we hold on to each other until Dad ends the call, sets the phone down, and rolls his chair back from the desk to face us.

I pull my hand from Mom's and drag a reading chair over to the desk and plop down on it.

"Where is she? Is she okay? What happened to her?"

The words pour out of me faster than I can contain them, my voice rising with each question. I sound like a raving madwoman, but my parents don't seem to notice. We've all been sick with worry about Tessa.

Mom reaches for a box of tissues and pulls a chair up next to mine. She nudges a tissue into my hand, then slides her arm around me. We're both crying now.

Dad pinches his fingers against his eyes and heaves a deep sigh, a tremendous burden lifted from his shoulders. It takes him a moment to answer, and I'm about to jump out of my chair and shake him if he doesn't say *something* soon.

He rubs a hand over his hair and his tear-filled eyes rest first on Mom, then on me. "She called—"

I slide to the end of the chair. "What do you mean, she called? Called who?"

Dad holds a hand up. "Let me finish, please."

I slide back and chew on a thumbnail to help me keep my mouth shut.

He continues. "She's in New Mexico."

"*New Mexico*? Wha—"

"Alli." This time it's from Mom. I chew on my lip instead.

"Yes, New Mexico."

Dad leans over and grabs a tissue from the box on Mom's

lap, then wipes his nose. "She's okay. Her parents and the police are with her now at the hospital."

"The *hospital?*" Even Mom can't help herself.

Dad nods and looks over at her. "Yes. They're just checking her over. Apparently, she was in bad shape when they went to pick her up. She called from a payphone in New Mexico this morning and the local police there picked her up and transported her to the hospital."

Dad glances my way, then looks back at Mom with an expression I take to mean he has more to say but doesn't want to say it in my presence.

"What happened, Dad? Was she kidnapped? Was it those guys from the party?" I ask.

He shakes his head. "I don't have any details, Alli. I'm sorry. That's all I know for now."

No one says anything for a minute while we sit and absorb the news.

It's been two months since anyone's heard from Tessa, and we've all been walking around carrying a mountain of tension and fear on our shoulders. The weight of the worry and wondering has been unbearable.

Every morning, I wake up to a dark cloud hanging over my head like a thick fog, and I can't shake it for most of my day.

A missing report was filed on Tessa, an investigation opened, flyers passed out all over town, pleas made on the news, and every other effort made that we could think of, with all the stops pulled out, to find Tessa.

The police even questioned several students at school about her whereabouts. But other than bringing the two guys from the party and the driver of the car that night in for questioning, the police had no other leads to go on.

All three guys admitted that they'd left with Tessa and had gone to another party that night, but all claimed to assume she'd left with someone else after arriving because they couldn't find her later that night.

It was suggested once again that she may have just run away, but I don't think anyone who knew her well believed that.

Dad stands and gathers Mom and me into his strong arms. I know he's feeling grateful for Tessa's safety and is probably feeling extra thankful to have his own daughter safe here with him.

Avery's away at a friend's house from church for the weekend, but I'm positive word is going to spread fast in our tight community. I expect a call from her within the next hour or two.

And I'm sure we'll have another family cry session when she does.

Chapter Thirty-Four

"Tessa, can I come in?"

There's a lump in my throat although I've practiced this scenario a hundred times in my mind.

Be strong, Alli. She doesn't need you falling apart right now.

Standing outside her bedroom door, I fight the urge to plow through the door and belly flop onto her bed just like old times.

Old times that feel like a lifetime ago.

A timid voice drifts from the other side of the door. It's so soft that, at first, I wonder if I just imagined it.

But I take my chances and ease the door open.

The room is dark, except for the remnants of the sunset filtering through the sheer curtain that hangs from the single window on the other side of the bed.

For a second, I don't see Tessa. She's not on the bed, where she's usually propped up with a fashion magazine or her laptop. My eyes drift to the desk by the window, but I only make out the silhouette of the spindles from her empty desk chair. I can't see further into the room without pushing the door open wider.

Maybe she's in the bathroom?

"You can come in."

I jerk back in surprise and hit my hand on the doorknob, sending the door flying open and a jolt of pain traveling up my forearm. I try to shake it off.

Nope, not in the bathroom.

A soft laugh comes from the far corner of the room.

"Boo," she says.

The little shaft of dwindling light from the window doesn't quite reach the corner, but I still make out Tessa sitting cross-legged on her beanbag chair, her body sunk into it like an old rubber ball with the air sucked out of it.

I start to move toward the bed to sit down, but then decide that's too far and opt to sit on the floor at her feet instead.

"Hey, girl," I say.

It's been so long since we've been alone together that I've forgotten how to start a conversation with her. We're just two strangers plowing through the verbal mud together.

"Hey, yourself."

The room grows darker, and I'm relieved when Tessa reaches up and pulls the chain on the floor lamp. A soft glow of light washes down on us.

As my eyes adjust to the light, more details come into focus. She's thin. Way thinner than I've ever seen her. Her nails are bitten down and raw. Tessa always had gorgeous, manicured nails and, for some odd reason, that detail bothers me more than the weight loss. I don't mean to stare, but I can't seem to help myself.

Then, my gaze drifts to her face.

She looks at me, but instead of the spirited twinkle in her eyes that's always been Tessa's trademark—the twinkle that could always convince me to join her in mischief—her eyes are hollow and empty, a fire dowsed by the reality of a devastating experience.

I hope she senses compassion on my face instead of pity, but she breaks away and looks down at her lap. I have no way of knowing what she's feeling from me.

Her long, auburn hair, once one of her best features and a color I was always jealous of, is frazzled and dull and pulled tightly across one shoulder.

She picks at the hem of her blouse with nervous fingers.

I know she feels uncomfortable, alienated . . . damaged. She doesn't have to say it; her body language screams it into the room.

"Tessa?" I wait for a response, but she doesn't look up or acknowledge me. "How are you doing? You okay?"

She keeps her eyes down, but her hands grow still on her lap. "How do you *think* I'm doing, Alli?" Her words are acidic, challenging.

I'm up to the challenge, though. I've been anticipating it for weeks.

"Honestly, Tessa, I have no idea how you're doing. I'm not even going to pretend to know. In fact, you don't even have to tell me anything if you don't want to. We can just sit here and say nothing, and I'd be okay with that."

Her fingers move to pick at the ends of her hair, her face a stone of pale ivory. I almost believe that if I reach out and touch her, she'd crumble into a thousand shards all over that beanbag chair.

Silence fills the room for several seconds, and I start to think she's going to take me up on the sitting in silence suggestion. I mentally prepare to prove myself to her and say nothing if that's what she needs.

"That's noble of you," she finally says. The words feel like gravel cutting into me.

"What do you mean, Tessa?"

"We were best friends for years, Alli." She pulls a strand of coarse hair loose and flicks it to the floor. "You don't have to say anything for me to know what you're thinking. I know you're dying for me to tell all the dirty details so you can gloat about how you told me so and feel justified that I got what I deserved after how I treated you."

Her accusation hits like a blow to my chest. Grief, denial, anger, and an ocean of other emotions I can't identify ping through my brain like electric shocks. I open my mouth to defend myself, to tell her how wrong she is, but that's what she predicts will happen.

Tessa wants—*expects*—a fight from me.

Taking a deep breath, I rein in my emotions and let her words flow past me. Tessa's hurting and wants me to hurt with her. It's been a hard lesson to learn, but I'm ready to do what I should've done months ago: be the friend that Tessa needs and show her unconditional love. Even if that means supporting her from afar.

"You're still my best friend, Tessa. Nothing justifies whatever happened to you, and I will *never* judge you for anything you've gone through. To be honest, Tessa, I owe *you* an apology. For everything. For basing our friendship on *what* you did instead of trying to understand the *why*." I sigh. "I knew that you were going through some hard stuff at home and that you were trying to find validation or, maybe, were just feeling restless with our friendship."

I take a moment to try and pull myself together. I'm failing miserably at it.

"Maybe I should've come to you. I don't know. I honestly just *don't know*. But it doesn't matter now. All that matters now is that we're here in this room together again. Something—"

My voice fails. I swallow and take a deep breath. "Something I wasn't sure we'd ever get to have again."

I start to reach for her hand but stop myself. I know it will be too much for her—too soon. I reach up and brush a tear away instead.

"Will you forgive me, Tessa?"

She looks at me, her hardened expression softening, and I get a glimpse of the old Tessa peeking at me from behind those haunted eyes.

"You were talking about me in that article you wrote about teenagers taking risks, weren't you?" she asks.

I blink in surprise. Not what I expected after pouring my heart out and asking for her forgiveness, but I'll take it.

"Oh, you read that article?" I grin. "Yeah. Was it that obvious?"

"Totally."

She smiles, but it never reaches her eyes. There's a lingering sadness that's going to take a long time and an ocean of smiles to heal.

"I'm sorry too, Alli. For everything."

A single tear trickles down her cheek, followed by a faint trail of black mascara.

Pulling the sleeve of my T-shirt down over my fist, I rise to my knees, lean toward her, and wipe her cheek with the edge of my sleeve.

A sudden rush of love and sorrow washes over me as I think about how God must feel when he washes away the dark marks that life has left on all of us, and I wish I could do the same for Tessa.

But I know that only God can do that for her.

I can love her—be her friend. But I can't dissolve her pain or scrub away the stains sin has left on her. But God can. And I hope the time will come when Tessa finds that out for herself.

Until then, I'll be right here to help her pick up the pieces of herself again. Something I've been trying to do myself for a long time.

Because that's what best friends are for, right?

Did You Enjoy This Book?

~

If you enjoyed this book, I hope that you will consider leaving a
review on Amazon. Reviews are so important to an author.
Even just a line or two can make a huge impact!

www.amazon.com/dp/B09XZ89TC9

Goodreads.com/Regina_Felty

Subscribe to Newsletter:
www.rlfelty.com/Newsletter

Also by Regina Felty

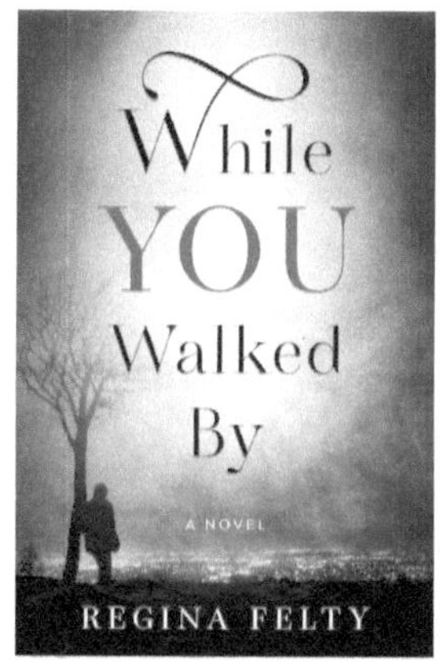
While
YOU
Walked
By
A NOVEL
REGINA FELTY

MAZIE
A NOVEL
REGINA FELTY